Second

A Practical Guide To Establishing Church Structure

Dr. Kirby Clements, Sr.

ISBN 0-917595-43-2

DEDICATION

To my wife, Sandra,
for her love, patience and encouragement.

ACKNOWLEDGEMENTS

I wish to thank Pastor Carolyn Driver for her encouragement and input during the revised phases of this project.

I wish to thank Pat Webb and Ann Stone for their diligent proofing of the text.

I wish to thank Janice Edgar, Ladi Otoki, Brenda Banks, and Charlotte Lemons for their technical assistance in fine-tuning this document in the computer.

I am especially grateful to Bishop Earl Paulk and the Presbyters of the "Cathedral of the Holy Spirit, Chapel Hill Harvester Church." Their contributions and support made this project possible.

TABLE OF CONTENTS

ABBREVIATIONS
And Their Meanings

Genesis . . . . Gen.
Exodus . . . . Exo.
Leviticus . . . . Lev.
Numbers . . . . Num.
Deuteronomy . . . . Deut.
Joshua . . . . Josh.
Ruth . . . . Ruth
1 Samuel . . . . . . 1 Sam.
2 Samuel . . . . . . 2 Sam.
1 King . . . . 1 Ki.
2 King . . . . 2 Ki.
1 Chronicles . . . . . 1 Chr.
2 Chronicles . . . . . 2 Chr.
Ezra . . . . Ez.
Nehemiah . . . . Neh.
Esther . . . . Est.
Job . . . . Psa.
Psalm . . . . Psa.
Proverbs . . . . Prov.
Ecclesiastes . . . . . . Ecc.
Song of Solomon . . . . Song
Isaiah . . . . Isa.
Jeremiah . . . . Jer.
Lamentations . . . . Lam.
Ezekiel . . . . Eze.
Daniel . . . . Dan.
Hosea . . . . Hos.
Joel . . . . Joel
Amos . . . . Am.
Obadiah . . . . Obad.
Jonah . . . . Jon.
Micah . . . . Mic.
Nahum . . . . Nah.
Habakkuk . . . . Hab.
Zephaniah . . . . Zeph.
Haggai . . . . Hag.

Zechariah . . . . Zech.
Malachi . . . . Mal.
Matthew . . . . Matt.
Mark . . . . Mk.
Luke . . . . Lk.
John . . . . Jn.
Acts . . . . Acts
Romans . . . . Rom.
1 Corinthians . . . . . 1 Cor.
2 Corinthians . . . . . 2 Cor.
Galatians . . . . Gal.
Ephesians . . . . Eph.
Philippians . . . . Phil.
Colossians . . . . Col.
1 Thessalonians . 1 Thessa.
2 Thessalonians . 2 Thessa.
1 Timothy . . . . 1 Tim.
2 Timothy . . . . 2 Tim.
Titus . . . . Tit.
Philemon . . . . Phile.
Hebrews . . . . Heb.
James . . . . Jam.
1 Peter . . . . 1 Pet.
2 Peter . . . . 2 Pet.
1 John . . . . 1 Jn.
2 John . . . . 2 Jn.
3 John . . . . 3 Jn.
Jude . . . . Jd.
Revelations . . . . Rev.

"There are four things which are little upon the earth, but they are exceedingly wise; the ants are a people not strong, yet they prepare their meat in summer; the conies are but a feeble folk, yet they make houses in the rocks; the locusts have no king, yet they go forth all of them in bands; the spider taketh hold with her hands, and is in king's palaces" (*Prov. 30:24-28*).

Every system of accomplishment exhibits some order, design and purpose. Order contends with chaos and is compatible with freedom. Design serves a gravitational function and establishes parameters of activity and expression. Purpose gives meaning to uncertainty. Visions are often hindered because of failure to maintain a proper tension between the directive forces of order, design and purpose and the dynamics of zeal and enthusiasm.

The *Second* is a compilation of experiences, observations and concepts concerning the cooperative relationship that must exist between primary leadership, associates and staff. Leaders should lead without unnecessary distractions. Associates and other staff members, as implementors, must comprehend their cooperative roles in the productive process. Since concepts are the genesis of behavior, there must exist some consistency in principles of government and ministry philosophy among visionaries and implementors. Hopefully, this book will explore that possibility.

CHAPTER 1
PHILOSOPHY OF MINISTRY

For any ministry to survive and to be successful there must be some common ground of belief shared between the leadership and support staff. The experiences and background of the organizational team may be varied but there must be some common gravitational norms that establish the boundaries, interests, performance levels, expectations and operational criteria for the overall group. Continuity and consistency in thought and performance can be shared by all the groups if there exists a common ministry philosophy. The consequences of the absence of such a ministry philosophy are equally convincing.

Ministry philosophy refers to principles, concepts and values used to make decisions, establish priorities, exercise influence or for deciding the effectiveness of a ministry. Lessons learned in life situations become the underlying assumptions that guide and motivate a leader and ultimately a staff.

All leaders operate from a ministry philosophy. Bishop Earl Paulk, Pastor of the 10,000-member Cathedral of the Holy Spirit, imparted to me one of his ministry philosophy ideas: Learn to put some things on the shelf of your mind and leave them there until another day; leave some things on the shelf forever. This principle has motivated me many times to systematically neglect the less urgent for the most urgent and to abandon concern over matters over which I have no direct control. Learning to establish priorities is the first principle of survival.

Through years of experience we develop value statements, critical assumptions, standards for ethical conduct and guidelines for the evaluation of ministry. Hopefully, all these are derived from Biblical principles. These principles are landmarks and have been proven to be enduring and fundamental. They are foundational truths that have universal application to individuals, groups, relationships and to any organization. When such principles are internalized, they become the basis of values, assumptions, conduct, attitude and behavior. And we should "...*Remove not the ancient landmarks, which the fathers have set . . .* " if we expect to experience the success of the fathers.

One striking lesson learned is that methods change but principles are constant. Therefore, at every level such a philosophy must honor Biblical principles. While there are many similarities between a ministry and a secular corporation, there exists basic differences. A ministry, rather than a corporation, must be based upon sound principles such as integrity, honesty, fairness, loyalty, faithfulness, excellence, patience, love and other foundational truths that are revealed in Scripture. Although a ministry must be open to the challenges of the times and accommodate the gifts and development level of people, the Bible must be the underlying foundation of its philosophy.

Ministry philosophy may be simplistic or complex, complete or in development; it may be quite extensive in its content. However, if the intended purpose of the ministry philosophy is to be realized it must be comprehended by the leaders and staff who function under its influence. People are much more effective when they know the parameters, values, goals and requirements of a ministry.

The following is a list of some areas where a ministry philosophy should be developed:

*		Spiritual discernment and decision making

*		Ministry values

*		Relationship with peers, superiors and subordinates

*		Crisis resolution

*		Leadership selection and development

*		Evaluation of effectiveness of ministry

*   Standards of ethical, moral and attitudinal conduct

Allow me to comment on the dynamics involved in some of these.

Spiritual Discernment and Decision Making

There are certain principles to be recognized when the Holy Spirit is given his rightful position as the executive administrator of the Church. He must have absolute power in the decision and direction of the ministry. Since the Spirit operates in total agreement with the Word, all the leaders and the people must constantly be grounded in the Word. Since in a multitude of counsel there is safety, the Holy Spirit should have the right to be heard among a plurality of elders in the decision making process.

Spiritual discernment and decision making is not some mystical or ethereal exercise void of reason or even common sense. In any ministry discernment and decision making should always be held in proper relationship with the Spirit, Word, faith, facts, and reality. Faith does not deny reality but rather bridges the gap between what exists and what has been promised. It is not wise to negate the obvious nor disregard facts. Sound decisions and spiritual discernment should not be made in a vacuum but in consideration of all factors.

Ministry Values

It is important to determine what motivates and controls a ministry. Crisis and the daily demands of people can direct a ministry and determine its priorities unless ministry values are determined. There is a tendency to protect and support that which is valued in a ministry by giving it priority status.

Sensitivity to the Holy Spirit is one of the most critical attributes of a ministry. To hear and obey the Holy Spirit is the life and strength of every ministry. Therefore, it is important to maintain an environment where the Holy Spirit has liberty to administrate without restraints. This freedom of the Holy Spirit is guarded by the character of the ministry. Integrity, honesty, fairness, love, patience, truthfulness, consistency, and faithfulness should be virtues pursued by all leaders in the discharge of their duties.

The most important commodity of a ministry is the people-not the buildings, property, missions or financial base. Concern for the spiritual and emotional welfare of the people must be a foremost consideration. Each person must be loved for whom they are and where they are.

The Great Commission is to proclaim the gospel and make disciples of all nations. This cannot be accomplished unless a strong home-based ministry is maintained. A healthy relationship must be maintained between outreach and inreach. Hence, the spiritual, emotional and physical welfare of the local ministry must be sustained (inreach) in order to facilitate evangelism (outreach).

In addition to evangelism, unity is important in any ministry. A mutual cooperation between members of the leadership team is necessary. There may be disagreement between leadership behind closed doors but there must always be a united front before the people. Disunity is a curse to any ministry.

Evangelistic directives and ministry priorities should not be established simply upon the availability of finances nor upon the needs of the people. Financial productivity and congregational consent should always be held in proper balance with the consenting opinion of the Holy Spirit which will come through leadership dedicated to prayer.

Relationship with Peers, Superiors and Subordinates

The basis of relationship between leadership, associates and staff can be supportive, protective, and instructive. The intended purpose of ministry relationships will determine the nature of the interaction. In a peer relationship (pastors to pastors) there is a mutual sharing of information with a greater level of vulnerability. Weakness and strengths can be shared without negative consequences.

Doubts, fears and emotions may be exchanged in such a mutually supportive and protective environment.

In a mentoring relationship with subordinates (pastor to new associate) the leader assumes a posture that is intended to provide nurturing, support and development. The mentor is expected to recognize the potential in an individual and provide the knowledge, guidance, challenges, and opportunities for experiences that will develop that potential. Such a relationship requires a mutual respect of all parties involved. The familiarity and vulnerability levels should be determined by the purpose of the relationship. A mentor cannot become one the "boys" or "girls" and maintain an instructive posture. Some distinctions should be made between peer relationships and those designed for mentoring.

Another critical factor in all of the relationships is trust. Mutual respect, honesty, fairness in evaluation, confidentiality and genuine communication will greatly contribute to the development of an environment of trust. Associates and staff will be honest and truthful in sharing information in an environment where telling the truth is welcomed. Leaders that are fair and honest in their appraisals of associates and staff send strong signals into the environment that they valued people for who they are and not simply for what they do.

Many ministry relationships are not healthy because of a breach of confidentiality. Unrestrained disclosure breeds disloyalty and damages the trust factor in any relationship.

In any ministry culture where the honest messenger is "shot" and publicly annihilated, accurate sharing of information will be greatly hindered. When telling the truth is considered a risk factor, people will only share what is "socially acceptable" or expedient. They wont's "rock the boat" or disagree nor tell the truth. The psychological factor of forced dishonesty is expressed in a gradual lowering of self esteem because the individuals violate their own personal integrity by not expressing what they truly feel.

When leaders are honest and disclose proper information to associates and staff the ministry environment is fortified with trust rather than suspicion. When leaders remove the mystery around what they feel and how they think, people have a better understanding of the leader's attitude, behavior and decisions.

Expectations should be clarified. Whenever people know what is required of them and the parameters within which they must function they can operate at a greater level of confidence and trust. Uncertainty pollutes the trust environment. Clear signals from leadership to staff will enhance the trust level.

Crisis Resolution

Crisis is inevitable in any ministry. A crisis may appear unexpectedly and disrupt the status quo. There may arise the need to "downsize" a staff or cut back on some ministry programs. But where should that first incision be made? In such instances the resolution of crisis demands decision making and problem solving in the light of the overall vision and values of the ministry. When the goals, objectives and values are clear and Biblical principles are applied, then the decisions and resolutions in times of crisis will maintain the integrity of the overall ministry. Priority status will be given to staff and functions that are necessary for the life of the ministry.

Leadership Selection and Development

The continuation of any ministry depends in part upon the ongoing recognition and nurturing of leadership. Therefore, the structure of the ministry should provide opportunity for young leaders to be identified and developed. Ministry outlets should be established that allow potential leadership to exercise gifts and callings. Mentoring programs should be initiated by the senior leadership to facilitate this process.

Young aspiring leaders should be taught how to respond to the Holy Spirit and the Word in making decisions, establishing priorities and resolving conflicts. They should be exposed to local leadership within the ministry and also to resources outside the local fellowship. It is important to recognize that leadership selection is not a democratic process dependant upon human will or initiative. This is not an equal opportunity process that gives everyone a chance. The importance of divine callings and giftings must be emphasized.

The demands and responsibilities of leadership must be clearly articulated to those called and chosen to enter into the ranks of servants. It is equally important that potential leaders be encouraged to express their expectations and ambitions.

Evaluation of Effectiveness of Ministry

The evaluation of the effectiveness of any ministry is usually measured by its achievements and annual growth. These are visible and measurable statistics and include such factors as congregational membership, size and condition of the physical plant, ministerial and auxiliary staff, television outreach, worship and arts program, intramural support programs, mission, outreach activities and financial budget. These variables seem to establish the "profitability" or "popularity" of a ministry. That is, the effectiveness of the ministry seems to be proportionate to its production. Consequently, local Churches are referred to by their statistics. However, there may be other factors that ought to be considered in the evaluation process.

Several years ago, our leadership staff was considering the continuation of television outreach. Cost of production and lack of financial returns were the major factors influencing our decision. The television programs were not specifically directed toward a general congregational audience but toward leadership. Although the average Christian viewer was greatly blessed and edified by the content of the programs, our target audience was the leaders of ministries. The financial returns from the programs were not sufficient to cover the cost factors. Hence, television was a mission endeavor of our local Church. As we gathered one morning to finalize the decision to cease programming, a prophetic word came from one of the elders declaring the spiritual profitability of the television outreach. We were exhorted to re-examine the effectiveness of the television ministry and to continue programming. The Holy Spirit had focused our attention upon another factor in the evaluation of a ministry -- spiritual profitability -- that is, the effectiveness of a ministry in fulfilling a spiritual directive without measurable statistics.

God had called Bishop Paulk's ministry to impact the Christian Church with the preaching and teaching of the Kingdom of God and the implication of such a message. The television outreach was a vehicle to expose the Holy Spirit's work among us in innovative ministry concepts, programs, musical and artistic expression, liturgy, and a trans-cultural congregation. Our local Church was a "storehouse" of spiritual goods expressed in tangible and visible giftings, callings and anointings. And the spiritual profitability of the ministry was determined by the degree of our faithfulness to a "heavenly vision." So it seemed good to the Holy Ghost (and to us) to continue with an outreach program that initially did not produce the tangible profits expected.

Today, television has been a most significant factor in the growth and continued exposure of our local ministry. Leaders both nationally and internationally still commend the impact of this ministry upon their work and lives. Interestingly enough, that impact came through television programming that we had considered discontinuing because it did not have statistical profitability.

This same principle can be applied in the evaluation of an overall ministry. Finances, congregational size, physical plant and other statistics are sometimes signs of growth. However, in the determination of the continuation of ministry it is also important not to neglect its significance in fulfilling a spiritual directive. Practical and measurable parameters should be considered in the evaluation process while being conscious of a transcending significance.

A well defined and articulated vision is an invaluable tool in the evaluation process. Vision is a compelling interest that captures attention. It is a gravitational force that navigates actions. When the central theme of a ministry is properly presented and given practical expression, it serves as a centripetal influence that can guide activities, establish priorities and directives and monitor the effectiveness of all aspects of the ministry. When the vision is kept in sight and in mind, the validating factor of effectiveness and profitability of any aspect of the ministry will be its support of that theme.

Standards of Ethical, Moral and Attitudinal Conduct

The attitude in which service is rendered is quite important. Attitude represents the mental condition, the feeling or emotional state of the individual. A major airlines has as motto: We love to fly and it shows! The slogan was very descriptive of the relationship that existed between service and the attitude in which that service was rendered. Some restaurants must certainly have as slogans: We don't like to serve and it shows! The lack of friendliness, kindness, and courtesy in some establishments negate the good quality of the food. Ministry is service oriented. The attitude in which that service is rendered is a validating factor. Perhaps a good ministry motto should be: We Love To Serve And It Shows!

In addition to attitudes, standards of ethics and morality must be Biblically based. Leadership and staff should set an example both in their public and private lives that can be emulated. Whatever structure is established to promote such standards should also provide for the restoration of those who fall short of its demands.

It is important in any pastorate that there be clarity and consistency in the overall concepts, ideas, purpose, and values of the ministry. Job descriptions for leadership and staff with specific guidelines and responsibilities can be most helpful in maintaining consistency in practice and concept. These are tools useful in guiding people in daily activities and can provide certain benefits:

*	Enable the leadership and staff to have a ministry-oriented reason to accept or reject a ministry opportunity that comes their way.

*	Give a precise understanding of strategies and tactics that are acceptable in the ministry.

*	Target the purpose of that leader or staff worker or ministry.

*	Establish criteria for the ongoing evaluation of that ministry.

*	Describe correct protocol in normal and crisis situation.

*   Identify the supervision of that staff or ministry.

Clear job descriptions and policies are invaluable in establishing and maintaining the integrity of a ministry. Christianity in America is increasingly coming under attack by civil government regulation and private litigation. The security of a ministry rests in its obedience to the purposes of God and the maintenance of some sense of consistency in practice and concept among all of its leadership and staff. A clear philosophy of ministry will be a definitive step in the right direction.

CHAPTER 2
PRINCIPLES OF LEADERSHIP

For any organization to survive and to be successful there must be a definitive leadership model. Such a leadership model may be plural with several elders or singular with an individual commander. Regardless of the size of the model, it must provide directions and establish parameters for those who will follow.

Leaders are pathfinders who are willing to make decisions and assume responsibility for others. If they are effective they will be able to elicit the trust and confidence of those who follow them. Capable leaders are motivators with an ability to guide others to higher level of performance and productivity. People are capable of great accomplishments whenever effective leaders enlist their participation.

Control and manipulation have negative connotations. Yet a leader must exert influence. One who leads must manipulate and control the work environment by having the willingness and persistence to ask the right questions consistently until the correct response comes forth, to set agendas for a whole group in order to facilitate the productive participation of that group, and to press for commitments and responses from people when they are operating below their natural and spiritual potentials.

A sense of pride and ego strength is in every leadership model. The effective leadership of others requires some self confidence and a sense of divine participation. In some younger leaders this may at times be displayed as a type of brashness, arrogance and even stubbornness while they wrestle over self identification and personal insecurities. Yet, if the ability to lead is not simply a matter of individual choice but one of divine selection and giftings, then some true confidence must come when the issue of election is settled. With time and experience, a leader will settle the internal conflicts surrounding calling and purpose, and a genuine sense of confidence -not arrogance, brashness nor stubbornness- will be exhibited.

Every leader will wrestle with insecurities. Perhaps this is due to the uncertainty over decisions, the hazard of having to trust people and the risk of being a messenger of divine revelation. Perhaps this is the natural tension that exist between confidence and the lack of it. The thought that a single decision could determine the course of an entire ministry or that dependency upon others could prove to be perilous at a critical moment can be the genesis of insecurity. Nevertheless, a conscious and sensitive awareness of our impotency without God is healthy.

Leaders are born and made. This is the issue of the chicken and the egg. Giftings seem to be inherent in the individual while the discipline to lead comes by experience. Some are natural motivators possessing intrinsic abilities which well adapts them to a forerunner function. There are other less gifted leaders who are able to function quite effectively.

While giftings are significant for leadership, personal discipline is the common denominator and the ultimate factor determining success. The willingness to exhibit self control and maintain personal integrity will be the yardstick of measurement. **Even a "born leader" has to become one.**

There are no distinct personality types, voice tone or physical stature that makes one leader more effective than another. Some leaders resemble and sound like giants while others are weak in stature and squeak. Some possess the persona of royalty, while others have the elegance of a bull in a china shop.

Some leaders are emotionally and physically able to handle the pressure and stress of their role more effectively than others. There seems to be different degrees of resiliency to the normal tension and demands of the role. However, all leaders seem to adapt to challenges in their own ways.

Leaders must maintain a healthy relationship between themselves and people they lead. Interaction with the people to form bonds of trust, love and friendship are necessary. However, close relationship with a congregation can breed familiarity and obligations that hamper the effectiveness of leadership. Leaders are not called to be friends of the people nor are they called to lord over them.

There are some qualities that seem to be consistent in effective leadership. Firstly, there is empathy and acceptance toward those they lead. This is the ability to project themselves into the lives of others and identify with their challenges. Secondly, there is a tolerance of imperfections. They can accept the abilities and performances of the individuals, though at times they may reject the products of their efforts. Effective leaders recognize the potential and limitation of people. Thirdly, they possess an awareness and sensitivity to the signals emitted by the people and environment. There is an intrinsic ability to discern the times, seasons, moods, and attitudes of people and the circumstances in which they encounter. And fourthly, there is the ability or willingness to adapt to change. Leaders are able to overhaul their psyches and replace basic assumptions, tactics, and methods with more effective tools when the occasion warrants such a response.

Leadership and Personality Dynamics

During my travels nationally and internationally, I have discovered that personality and leadership styles are related . The personality type seems to influence the method of leadership. Starting with the four basic personality types -- Choleric (energetic, controlling), Sanguine (warm, charming), Melancholy (analytical, perfectionist), and Phlegmatic (easy-going, submissive) -- there is an obvious association between the way an individual relates to the environment and the behavioral and emotional tendencies of an individual. In a plural leadership mode consisting of primal and associate functions, such understanding of personality and response relationships would be helpful.

The following is a limited sample of some personality and leadership characteristics:

Type 1 Personalty (Sanguine): This type is hearty and optimistic yet tender with an ability to share in the emotions of others. They are generally outgoing, friendly and spontaneous.

Sanguines are tremendous motivators, great starters, but not so great as a finisher. They demand allegiance and full cooperation from associates. Sanguines will generally make instant decisions and handle challenges courageously. They need achievement and appreciation.

Type 2 Personalty (Choleric): This type is aggressive, tenacious, self-confident with a singleness of purpose. Cholerics tend to be keen organizers and good at appraising situations. They are forceful, dominant and rule with an iron hand. They can be blunt, sarcastic, unsympathetic and slow to show approval. Cholerics are capable of challenging dissonance, but they can learn to entreat.

Type 3 Personalty (Melancholy): This type is sensitive and creative. They are emotional, analytical, and detailed. Melancholics tend to be perfectionists and can be very demanding of themselves and others. They are often indecisive for fear of making mistakes. They disdain confrontation, chaos and tend to entreat others.

Type 4 Personalty (Phlegmatic): This type is easygoing, good-natured, very practical and tenacious. Phlegmatics are quiet and undemanding. They rarely make sudden decisions and are good organizer. They need respect and a feeling of worth.

A Choleric senior pastor could not understand why a Melancholy youth leader made good plans on paper but was reluctant to give commands and implement the process quickly. Cholerics are born leaders and need to see agendas accomplished. While a Melancholy is writing and planning on paper, the Choleric has organized the whole affair and is busy giving orders to everyone in sight.

The desire of the Phlegmatic is to keep peace. When this is not possible, the Phlegmatic will sometimes emotionally withdraw and refuse communication until some order is restored. A Sanguine leader could not understand his Phlegmatic administrator's lack of responsiveness during one of their emotionally tensed presbytery meetings. A Phlegmatic will retreat rather than confront the enemy. Because Phlegmatics desire peace and long for respect, a Sanguine leader may mistake their lack of enthusiasm and zeal as either rebellion or disagreement.

A Choleric associate was quite upset about his Sanguine leader. The associate had assessed all of the strengths and weaknesses of the leader and felt capable of doing the job better than the leader. This Choleric had a top position as a chief associate but was upset over having to be the second without any possibility of being in charge.

During a period of transition, a Church was undergoing a decentralization of the leadership function. With the increase in congregational size came a need for additional leaders and staff. The Melancholic administrator was elated over the possibility of additional support that would bring order and design to the confusion created by a leadership void. The Choleric leader was threatened over the decentralization of authority and the possible loss of some control. The Phlegmatic associate was deliberating the cost factors and encouraging a gradual addition. The Sanguine chief musician was not obviously concerned with the discussion at all, but was rather preoccupied with the plans for an upcoming musical presentation.

I recall an instance when three local pastors decided to combine their fellowships and meet in one facility. The memberships were excited about the merger and the prospects of a single larger Church. It was decided that the pastor with the larger fellowship should serve as the primal leader and the other pastors as associates. The congregations adapted quite well. The pastors decided that all decisions would be a joint venture between the three of them. All went well for about six months until it was discovered that one of the associates was making independent decisions apart from the other two pastors. The associate was the hearty and optimistic type who is very outgoing, friendly and spontaneous. He earnestly wanted to be a team player, and his motive was to help build the corporate Church. But he was spontaneous, friendly, and the young people of the Church were attracted by his ministry. The other two pastors thought that his actions were divisive and rebellious. By the time that I visited the Church they were ready for a two-way split. In a meeting with the three pastors we discussed the problem with each one giving their perspective and possible solution. We eventually began to talk about the personality dynamics of the plural pastorate and of each individual pastor. The senior pastor was obviously the aggressive, tenacious and self-confident type who rules with an iron hand. It was important to him to be aware of all decisions and activities. Because he demanded allegiance and full cooperation from associates, he viewed anything less than that to be rebellion and disloyalty. The associate who seemed to be on good term with the primal leader was the easy-going, good-natured type who was obviously very practical and a good organizer. He rarely made sudden decisions and tended to bounce his ideas off the primal leader. But the prodigal associate was the spontaneous one. He was part of a team of one who needed to be in charge and another who needed respect. The three of them did not change any personalities, but they did agree that the conflicts were not a matter of divisiveness nor rebellion. And they did agree that communication was a challenge since each of them had once been autonomous decision-makers in their own ministry. But they also consented to communicate.

Obviously, these few examples do not in anyway exhaust the many different personality/relationship modes. Yet, they do draw attention to factors that can contribute to a more profitable relationship between primal leaders, associates, and staff.

The Significance of Trust and Honesty

Success in a work environment depends upon integrity and communication. When promises are kept and there is obvious equity in the appraisal of people, motivation runs high. Healthy environments that are brisk with a sense of fairness, honesty, and mutual caring will promote a greater level of individual participation and productivity. Too many closed doors, lack of information - sharing, will foster a climate of insecurity and fear. People need to feel like part of the family. Emotional feeling of being included in the "pact" promotes self esteem and personal worth. It is vital for the work week to be punctuated with good communication periods that encourage participation of associates and staff. Whenever people are emotionally and intellectually included in the decision-making process, it increases loyalty and a sense of belonging.

In addition, people need to be affirmed. Genuine endorsement and recognition for a job well done, a note of congratulation or a few words of praise in the presence of peers builds self-esteem. Appropriate recognition reinforces messages of success to any individual. Whenever a good performance is rewarded there is a reinforcement of such profitable behavior.

The converse also works quite effectively. If genuine affirmation reinforces performance then surely lack of any commendation for a job well done will bring about extinction. Affirmation sends a positive signal to an individual that their performance is acceptable. Lack of any commendation sends a message that their behavior or performance is unacceptable. Effective leadership will recognize the time to affirm and/or to correct. Whenever people are constantly bombarded with critical and judgmental evaluation of their performances without appropriate commendation it fosters a sense of hopelessness and failure.

I was invited to a meeting of the ministers and staff of a large Church. The senior pastor was very articulate and a good listener. He was quick to share credit with his associates and staff and gave honest appraisal for their performances. There existed a healthy balance between the negative and positive commendations. Although his authority was quite obvious, he exhibited an ability to help everyone in the ministry feel good about themselves. His words and action enhanced the self-esteem of the staff and increased their willingness to share ideas openly. There was a sense of shared responsibility without competitiveness.

There is a time to be intolerant of differences and stubborn towards the resistance to anything that threatens to undermine the foundations of a Biblical mission. There is a time to ask the right questions and offer alternative solutions that manipulate an action or a decision in a desired direction. However, for information to be accurately shared between leaders and staff an environment must be created where honesty is rewarded. When people are annihilated for telling the truth then honesty will be viewed as a risk factor. It is not good to shoot the honest messenger. Many staff meetings are a waste of time because an environment has been created that fosters being "socially acceptable" rather than honest. Such terms as "Don't rock the boat" or "Guard yourself" are indicative of culture where honesty is viewed as risky business. Whenever people are reluctant to be honest there is a decrease in accurate sharing of information, lower productivity and loss of personal integrity.

Primal leaders need associates who are honest and open about their ideas and concepts. There is safety in a plurality of sincere and honest counsel. No effective leader desires to be totally controlled by personal opinions and desires. However, strong leaders can become so intolerant of differences in opinions from among their associates and staff that they stifle the creativity and honesty of their support base. Associates and staff can become so self-protecting of their reputation and their need of approval that they compromise the integrity of their opinions and ideas. A differing opinion of an associate or staff member with a primal leader is not always a sign of disloyalty or betrayal. There can be disagreement without antagonism. The greater danger lies in false agreement for therein lies a violation of the confidence to be honest. Honest communication between primal leadership, associates, and staff must be nurtured.

When there is a healthy environment of trust and respect there can be open and honest interchange without fear of reprisal. On the other hand, when there is an environment of distrust and fear, associates and staff will generally become dishonest in their opinions and ideas for fear of reprisal or rejection. For example, there is a story recorded in *1 King 22:1-28* of two kings, Ahab and Jehoshaphat, who are preparing for war against Syria. Jehoshaphat asked the king of Israel to enquire at the word of the Lord for counsel regarding the war. Now Ahab had surrounded himself with false prophets of Baal. They were false prophets because they neither heard from God, nor were they sent by God. Consequently, they were self-serving, valued their reputation with the king of Israel, and always said good things to him. When Ahab asked counsel of these four hundred men concerning the battle against Ramoth-Gilead, they all consented and promised victory. Jehoshaphat did not trust the prophetic consensus of these men and asked for another prophetic opinion. Ahab sent for a prophet of the Lord named Micaiah whose reputation he stated in a few words: "I hate him since he doth not prophesy good concerning me, but evil." Micaiah is encouraged by the other false prophets to be in agreement with their counsel. He initially consents and gives a "good word." But, the "good word" violates Micaiah's own prophetic integrity and evokes rebuke from Ahab for its dishonesty. Micaiah recants and eventually gives a true word of prophecy at the expense of his own personal reputation with the other prophets and the king. This is a classic example to amplify the obligation of associates and staff to maintain honesty and integrity in their representation of counsel at the expense of their own reputation. One can be true and open with their opinions and ideas with a right spirit. Failure of associates and staff to be honest and open is to violate the trust invested in them by their primal leadership. Dishonesty or the withholding of information may be the highest level of betrayal.

Submission of an associate and staff to a primal leader simply means following instructions. It is not an abdication of the right of choice nor an attitude of agreement. True submission is the highest level of honesty and integrity since personal benefits are subordinated to reflect the character of the Lord Jesus. It is erroneous to confuse submission with the subordination of personal views for the sake of unity. True unity is borne out of truthfulness and genuine submission is demonstrated by honesty and personal integrity.

Delegated Leadership

As any ministry or organization grows there develops a need for more support to facilitate the process of service. This delegation of function and responsibility is a critical process. The admonition of the Apostle Paul not to "lay hands suddenly on any man," is a noteworthy remembrance during the process. The Lord Jesus is recorded to have prayed all night before He selected the twelve disciples *(Luke 6:12-13)*.

It is advisable to plan for the deputizing of other leaders. The crisis of need does not provide a very healthy environment for rash, unplanned decisions. If the "scouting" and identification of future leadership becomes a lifelong habit of senior leaders, then the selection process can be more accurate.

For example, the initiation of the diaconate as recorded in Acts 6 occurred seemingly because the growing demands of the work had exceeded the ability of the apostles. There was negligence in the daily ministration to the widows, and disputes and murmuring between the Grecians and Hebrews began to escalate. A classical sign of a need to delegate leadership function into the hands of others is the obvious lack of existing leadership to meet the needs. Murmuring by the people over the lack of availability of leadership is potentially a dangerous sign. If it is not addressed, false leadership will arise to solve the problem. So the apostles initiated the first recorded selection of deacons in the early Church *(Acts 6:1-7)*.

Associate leadership may include pastors, elders, deacons, deaconesses, administrators, ministries of helps and so forth. Such associates may possess talents and giftings unlike those of the primal leadership. This is complementary since it supplements the strengths and compensates for the weaknesses in the existing leadership model. It is a practical move to enlist associates who meet the ministry's weaknesses, or non-giftings, rather than the ministry's strengths. Of course, this can be threatening to the integrity of the ministry unless associates recognize that their position is to augment the effectiveness of the primal leadership model.

A senior pastor related to me a very interesting principle. He had experienced significant growth in the size of the congregation. The demands of the ministry required him to release more of the administrative responsibility to an administrative secretary. The delegation of administrative functions seemed to be so effective that the senior pastor completely abdicated all administrative responsibility. The administrative secretary became so proficient at "running" the Church that the pastor began to lose contact with the staff and the day to day cares of the ministry. When he did attempt to make an administrative decision he discovered that there existed a significant allegiance of the staff to the administrative secretary. He had over delegated responsibility and failed to maintain oversight and contact with the staff. Fortunately, the condition was corrected in time to avoid a potential crisis.

Senior leaders should be aware of over delegating responsibilities. Whenever associates are forced to become autonomous because of excess authorization by senior leadership there will be conflict. It is advisable for senior leaders to maintain communication with the ministration and administration function. It is also recommended that associates help facilitate communication with senior leaders in order to avoid confusion.

Part of the success of a ministry rests upon the ability of the key leader(s) to lead without distractions, especially from associates. Consequently, it is important for the associates to direct the focus of the people toward the primal leader(s) in the exercise of their ministry. Associates should never allow themselves to be placed in a competitive posture. Competition at leadership levels forces people to make choices in their allegiance. This is not healthy to any ministry.

Associates should discourage any comparison of the leadership among the people. If the integrity of the leadership is to be maintained, it is important that associates and senior leaders be aware of such comparisons. It was such a comparison of David and Saul among the people that possibly initiated a cloud of dissension and jealousy *(1 Samuel 29.5)*. During one of my visits to a thriving fellowship, I encountered such a situation. The plural leadership consisted of senior pastors and several associates. During the worship service several of the associates assumed responsibility for the announcements, congregational singing and prayers and the tithes and offerings. One of the young men was very articulate and seemed to elicit quite a response from the congregation whenever he came before them. After the service he asked to speak privately with me. He expressed his frustration over lack of opportunity to preach and that many members of the congregations had expressed their desire to hear him more often. We discussed at length his calling, ambition and expectation in that local assembly. It appeared that the private and public encouragement from the congregation had lit the flame of frustration. I encouraged a discussion with the senior pastor and the matter was favorably resolved.

Associate ministers who are gifted with effective preaching tools should be giving opportunities to express such a ministry. One senior pastor was in the process of adding a very gifted minister to his staff. The new associate was a former senior pastor and a very effective communicator. A key factor in such staff additions is to determine the need of the Church and the giftings of the potential candidate. If the need is for more assistance in preaching and teaching, then the addition of a gifted preacher or teacher will enhance the ministry. But if the need is for someone to assist in the worship service and relieve the senior pastor of visitation and counseling responsibilities, the addition of a minister desirous to preach and teach will eventually become a source of frustration. It is not desirous to add an associate to a pastoral staff whose ambition is to be a senior pastor unless there is a clear understanding and provisions are made for the accomplishment of that goal in the near future.

Many Churches serve as training ground for the development of future leaders. Some ministries provide a refuge for the rehabilitation of leaders with the hope of a future release of that minister. A primal leader would do well to view such associates as transitional resources and expect a future release of such ministries. A senior pastor related to me how a young musician had joined his local Church for the purpose of rehabilitation. The musician was very gifted and so willing to assist in the Church that eventually an entire music team had evolved around his leadership. The senior pastor was quite aware that the tenure of this young musician would be temporary. Instead of leaning up the ability of the young musician to teach and train others, the musician lead all the congregational singing and sang the majority of the musical selections. When the young man did leave, it created an obvious deficit.

Expectations, ambitions and giftings of associates in a plural leadership should be examined and discussed without fear. A senior leader shared with me his surprise over the resignation of the youth pastor. Here was a young man who had served as the head of the Youth Department for seven years and offered his resignation without any prior notice. When the senior pastor did meet with the young leader, the desires and ministry expectations were exposed. The youth leader had served seven years with the expectation of becoming the senior pastor of that local Church or some other ministry. Although no such promises had ever been given to the young leader, assumptions had been made and expectations had grown. This incidence is not too unlike Jacob serving Laban seven years for

Rachel. (The difference lies in the fact that the promise of Laban and the expectation of Jacob were quite clear even though deception was near at hand.)

An effective primal leader should be aware that some of the desires of an associate may develop after several years of service. In many instances the evolution of ministries within a local Church may serve as a catalyst. Honest and open communication about the expectations and desires of associates and the ability of the local Church to fulfill them can often avert a leadership crisis.

Leadership in the Pew

The threat of losing integrity and continuity looms over any ministry, especially in a period of growth when adding staff. The decentralization of leadership demands adding associates who may lack the experience of the founding leaders and who possess gifts and callings that may appear to be different. New ministry modules become necessary such as care groups or home cell groups. Volunteers become necessary to handle the growing needs among the youth, elderly, singles, single parents, and young families. Each new support ministry potentially becomes a new channel of influence and authority within the overall Church. Yet, these can potentially function as a tremendous resource to a ministry if they are managed properly with clear guidelines and appropriate checks and balances. New members classes are very helpful in orienting potential volunteers. Strategically scheduled staff meetings for briefing, interdepartmental sharing, and prayer can provide an opportunity for leadership to impart directives and strategies.

Several years ago our leadership recognized the need for additional shepherding resources. We knew the homes were a very obvious place for ministry. The Scriptures are replete with examples of the ministry of Jesus and the disciples in the homes of the people *(Luke 8:51-55; Mark 1:29-34; Luke 6:12-13, 7:36-48, 9:4, 10:5-7)*. So our leadership began to divide the entire Church congregation into geographic zones based upon postal zip codes. Each associate pastor was assigned a specific number of zip code areas. Deacons and deaconesses would work with the associate pastor to develop home care groups within certain strategic zip code areas. Specific guidelines were given in order to maintain continuity. The groups were to be evangelistic and seek to enlist the participation of residents in the community of the care group. These groups were not to become Bible studies, nor small Churches. There was a healthy growth among most of the groups and people were added to the Church through them.

We discovered something very interesting during those phases. If the pulpit is viewed as the most significant facet of the ministry, it becomes a goal for others to pursue. Jesus addressed the issue of "greatness" after a dispute among the disciples over the issue of preeminence. Greatness was something attainable by all who would serve. It was never associated with a position or office - only with an attitude. The pew and the pulpit must be viewed with a proper paradigm and given the significance ascribed to them in the Scriptures. For instances, the Church is a body of believers. Leaders exist to equip the saints to do the work of the ministry *(Ephesians 4:11-13)*.

The division between leaders and the congregations is based upon gifting and function and not upon arbitrary selection. The distinction is one of a divine origin. The Apostle Paul makes this point quite clear in the explanation of the Church as a body with many members possessing different functions *(I Corinthians 12:4-31)*. The arm does not attempt to perform the function of the foot nor does the ear seek to speak. The "scandal of particularity," as it has been called, is that God chooses and equips. An event happens here and not there, now and not then, to this person and not to that. Even though gifts are given to different members of this body there is no hierarchy nor competitiveness. That is precisely what the Apostle Paul conveyed to the Corinthian Church in a rhetorical question: "Are all apostles? are all prophets? are all teacher? are all workers of miracles? Have all the gifts of healing? do all speak with tongues? do all interpret?"

When this body of members assembles, there can be no striving for preeminence. There is no particular gift nor function that is more important than another. The pulpit is not more significant than the pew. The occupant of the pulpit may perform the function of speaking the word of God; but without the recipient sitting in the pew, there will be no productivity of the word spoken. If the pulpit is viewed as the "treasure" to be earned, then congregants, deacons, deaconesses and care givers will serve with the motivation of one day attaining the pulpit. I dare say that this misconception exists to some degree in the Churches.

The Dynamics of Gifting and Function

Whenever ministry distinctions are made based upon function and giftings, most misconceptions concerning the pulpit ministry are eradicated. "Function" is the action or purpose for which a person is particularly designed or suited. "Gifting" is the inherent capacity, talent or aptitude of the person. Gifting determines function.

In a ministry environment, function may often be observed before the identification of the gifting is established. How often we observe an individual repeatedly performing certain tasks before we identify the giftings. In fact, an individual's gifting and function may be discovered while performing tasks not directly related to their calling. This may very well be a matter of semantics but the principle to be established is that distinctions, not hierarchy, should be based upon function and gifting.

As ministry continues to expand and the decentralization of leadership occurs, there is a danger of over-delegation as well as under-delegation. A reluctant leader can easily relinquish the undesirable chores to such an extent that the leadership image is diminished. The Moses and Jethro model of leadership is one upon which many ministries delegate responsibility. Jethro encouraged Moses to teach the people ordinances and laws and show them how to walk in obedience to those statutes. The next order of business was the delegation of able associates or counselors to judge the people. But Moses still participated in that function of leadership (Exodus 18). I was discussing this principle of over-delegation to a group of leaders and one among them made an interesting observation. This particular leader established a counseling department in the Church and delegated all of the counseling to a staff. He justified his position upon the premise that counseling was like leaving the word of God to wait upon tables. Other leaders in attendance echoed the same sentiment. We all agreed that counseling is not simply a shepherding function relegated solely to the pastor. However, I saw a potential danger in the over-delegation of this function. For instance, the counseling room is an environment that demands vulnerability and confidentiality. Counselees generally develop strong allegiances and even dependency upon counselors because of the help that they receive during times of personal crisis. If the counseling department is separated from the pastorate or the main stream of leadership, unnecessary fragmentation is prone to occur. This is not to negate a counseling department, but it is an expressed suggestion that primal leadership maintain healthy communication and involvement with those who function in the counseling gift.

The same principle of over-delegation can work in the home cell group concept. Primal leaders can be consistently absent and never visit the homes. Such a lack creates a continuity-void. An occasional visit to the home groups by a primal leader and frequent meetings with the home group leaders can generally ward off a potential breach of unity.

Sunday Morning Unity

When musician and worship leadership are added to a growing Church, an interesting challenge evolves. Leadership functioning in the capacity of praise and worship must quickly recognize that their primary responsibility is to establish an "environment" or "climate" conducive to the interaction of God and His people. Worship leaders are also called to facilitate a sense of unity with the primal leadership. Because of the public visibility of such leadership, independence or flaunting of talents pose a tremendous threat to any sense of unity, which alters the spiritual climate. I have been in Churches where musicians are autonomous and have no cooperative relationship with the primal leadership during a worship service. Some primal leaders can be so dominating that they stifle any creativity or freedom among the musicians, but freedom and creativity can be misused as license to transcend cooperative ministry. One particular Church that I visited had a tremendously gifted musical department; the musicians and singers were very talented. And the congregation responded enthusiastically to their vast repertoire. There were, however, several problems. First, the people were made to stand on their feet for an hour or more during the singing creating obvious fatigue. Secondly, there was an obvious lack of communication between the musicians and the pastor during the service. Thirdly, there seemed to be more of a response of the musicians to the consensus of the congregation rather than a sensitivity to the direction of the Holy Spirit.

Perhaps the solution to such challenges in these areas rest in our theology of worship. If worship is viewed as a re-enactment of the relationship that exists between God and His people, then whatever is done must be rooted in biblical, historical, redemptive events. This re-enactment of what God has done through Christ can be done through singing of hymns, spiritual songs, and other forms of music. But it can also be done through preaching, reciting of creeds, and prayers. The full spectrum of worship cannot be circumscribed within the limits of music alone. Nor can the full dimension of the worship experience be limited to preaching or teaching of the Word.

If worship is a re-enactment of events rooted in Scripture, it cannot be thrown together in a haphazard manner. During worship, the believers are aligned with Christ. The worship experience is designed to bring about a dynamic and living encounter between God and His people. Therefore, the supreme factor in worship is not the excitement nor the recreational process, but a vital encounter with God. For that reason, the ingredients and the structuring of worship cannot be subjected to the desires of creative artisans nor to public opinions. There must remain a delicate balance between creativity, Spirit, and the Scriptures. Thus those who lead or organize the ingredients of worship must be sensitive to the Spirit, the Word, and the people.

Music is, indeed, a vital part of the worship experience. It creates an environment and opens the heart of the people to hear the Word of God while preparing the heart of the speaker to declare the Word. For that reason, there can be no competition between music and the Word. There must exist a healthy relationship between the congregational praise and singing and the ministry of the Word of God. For the Word is not only preached or taught but it is delivered through the idiom of music. The key issue is sensitivity to the spiritual dynamics of the gathering of God's people; for ultimately, our theology will be reflected in our performance and preferences and the use of time.

Concept of A Corporate Anointing

A word needs to be spoken here about corporate anointing. For the sake of definition let us define "anointing" as the setting apart for an office or function and the validating presence or enabling of the Holy Ghost *(John 14:16,23; 1 John 2:27)*. The anointing is the freedom of the Holy Spirit acting upon an individual or a group. The Prophet Isaiah declared that: "*The Spirit of the Lord is upon me; because the Lord hath anointed me to preach good tidings unto the meek; he hath sent me to bind up the brokenhearted, to proclaim liberty to the captives, and the opening of the prison to them that are bound; to proclaim the acceptable year of the Lord and the day of vengeance of our God; to comfort all that mourn; to appoint unto them that mourn in Zion, to give unto them beauty for ashes, the oil of joy for mourning, the garment of praise for the spirit of heaviness; that they might be called trees of righteousness, the planting of the Lord, that He might be glorified*" *(Isaiah 61:1-3)*. The anointing was a testimony of the presence of the Holy Ghost and it was with purpose. The prophet stated the purpose clearly: "That He might be glorified."

An anointing can abide within an individual or a group of individuals. We have seen numerous examples of "individual anointing". Leaders such as Martin Luther, John Wesley, William Seymour, Oral Roberts, Kathryn Kuhlman, Aimee Semple McPherson, and many others were enabled by the Holy Spirit. But there are examples of "corporate anointings". Israel was anointed as a people of God's own choosing. The Church as the body of Christ is anointed as a corporate unity. In fact the Church's effectiveness in the world is to some degree based upon its corporate unity *(John 17:20-23)*. A team of leaders may be anointed to work together to perform a certain task. A local Church and its leadership can function under a corporate anointing and achieve exploits that it never could attain if fragmented into several smaller ministries. A musician can function under a corporate anointing and be quite effective as part of a local Church leadership team. Yet that same musician can lack a similar measure of success when functioning apart from the group. Success as part of a corporate body does not always guarantee the same anointing when functioning alone.

This same principle applies to any of the five-fold ministry gifts. There are occasions where an associate may function quite effectively as part of a team and lose that same effectiveness when functioning alone. The Church universal and local is "fitly joined together." Christ has given to the Church trans-local and local leadership *(Ephesians 4:11)*. There should be a sense of divine design in the building of a ministry. If that is so, then a leadership team cannot simply decide to fragment based upon any reason short of a divine initiative. A member of the team cannot decide to leave except it is initiated by the Holy Spirit *(Acts 13:1-3)*. Unfortunately, there are instances where a distrusting environment promotes interpersonal conflicts that results in associates leaving or being forced to leave.

Within a local Church, there may exist a plurality of elders who are resident in and appointed over that particular congregation *(1 Thessa. 5:12; I Tim. 5:17; Heb. 13.7)*. There are several ministries set in the Church with particular authority: "first apostles, secondarily prophets, thirdly teachers. . ." *(1 Cor. 12:28)*. Individuals with these ministries serve in a plural leadership together with other local elders, but they also function in a specific capacity as the Holy Ghost directs. Peter was an apostle, yet when writing to the elders, he refers to himself as a co-elder among them *(1 Pet. 5:1)*. Without losing the authority as an apostle, Peter also functioned in the office of an elder. There existed a recognition of a plurality of elders in the matter of government while acknowledging the particular ministry of the apostle, prophet, and teacher.

The ministry of the evangelist is mentioned by Paul in Ephesians 4:11 but excluded by name in *1 Cor. 12:28.* This ministry, by its nature, functions as an outside extension of the local Church (Acts 8:5-13, 26-40). Paul does not list "pastors" in I Corinthians 12:28, but they are included in the governing body of elders in the local Church *(Acts 20:17,28; Eph.4:11)*.

Wherever there exists a plurality of elders in a local assembly, there exist a diversity of functions and giftings. There is no corporate hierarchy of apostles as chief executive officers, prophets as administrative assistants nor pastors as supervisors. Sometimes this is interpreted to say that "the apostle hears it, the prophet speaks it, the teacher explains it, and the pastor gets it done." There should be no sense of spiritual descendancy in the local Church where one gift is more valued than another. The issue is gifting and function, not hierarchy. The body is "fitly joined together," and the office of apostle, prophet, evangelist, pastor, and teacher serve a definitive role. There is a danger in attempting to limit the function of the ascension gift ministers. To say that only the apostles can understand structure and govern or that only prophets can prophesy and guide is an extreme position. Such a concept would limit the leadership of a Church, organization or ministerial association to the apostles only. No instances exist in the New Testament where distinctions are made regarding the position that some of the five-fold ministers can hold in the Church. There are general instructions regarding the qualifications and standards *(1 Tim. 3:1-13; Titus 1:5-9)*. All of the five-fold ministers are expected to guide, govern, and instruct the people of God.

In some assemblies, apostles and prophets exercise authority over local pastors. This concept of government seems to be based upon Biblical references that apostles from Jerusalem exercised authority in the newly formed Church in Samaria *(Acts 8:14-25)*; prophets from Jerusalem exercised authority in Antioch (Acts 11:27-30); prophets and teachers in Antioch ordained apostles to go out to other areas, and they in turn ordained elders in various cities *(Acts 13:1-4; 14:23)*; and again apostles and elders in Jerusalem exercised authority in Antioch through the ministry of Judas and Silas *(Acts 15:23-3)*. However, the exercising of such authority was not an ecclesiastical autonomy. There was the issue of interdependence. All of the five-fold ministries offices recognized one another, received one another, and submitted to one another. The apostle recognized and submitted to the pastor, and the evangelist and prophet acknowledged and submitted to the ministry of the teacher.

If in a local assembly the apostle or prophet is not the pastor or the leader of the plurality of elders, who directs the Church? Can an apostle or prophet function in a cooperative and supportive role in a local assembly with the leading elder being a pastor? The answer to both of these questions rest again upon the recognition of giftings and functions. Whenever a plurality of leadership in a local Church is established, the Holy Spirit will impart to one of the leaders a charisma for leading or ruling. This is a special endowment for administration and direction within the collective leadership. It is the responsibility of all the elders in the local assembly to recognize this endowment and to submit to it. Such an individual may serve as the spokesman or representative of the whole group. This does not negate the collaborative function of the whole group of leaders. In the conference described in *Acts 15:1-29,* it seemed that the endowment of direction rested upon James the apostle. Nevertheless, the final decision was a corporate one expressed in the words, "It seemed good to the Holy Ghost, and to us. . .." In short, it was a unanimity among the whole group being expressed by the ministry of James. Every plurality of leaders must of necessity acknowledge a singular leader. The proverbial saying is true: "Anything with two heads is a monster."

The Challenges of Leadership

As earlier stated Bishop Earl Paulk, my mentor in ministry, has related to me many truths which have sustained him for well over fifty years in the ministry. With a 12,000 member congregation and 200 networking Churches, he has learned that a primary truth is to establish priorities. As I have previously said he advocates a systematic neglect of the less important for the urgent. Learning to put some things on the shelf of the mind until another day means survival. Some things you leave on the shelf forever.

The willingness to withdraw oneself from pressing pursuits and challenges in order to reorient priorities spells survival. Probably more poor decisions are made because of exhaustion and mental fatigue than is necessary. One leader shared with me his inability to separate himself from the work for a vacation because of guilt and fear that the project would collapse without him. Guilt and the pressure to perform are not good motivators. One young pastor shared with me her fear of failure as a driving force to perform. An associate was emulating his mentor's work ethic and suffered a collapse. The mentor's personality had scripted him to recover quicker from challenges with a short interval of rest; consequently, he rarely separated himself from his work. The young associate was not psychologically endowed to handle stress in the same manner. He suffered emotional fatigue because of a lack of reasonable rest. Each individual must understand his/her personal limitations and performance levels.

When a leader is functioning in his/her true calling, there is no emotional burnout. Burnout comes as a consequence of assuming responsibilities beyond one's designated calling. The apostles called for deacons to handle the daily ministrations of the people in order to give themselves to prayer and study of the word *(Acts 6.1-6)*. How often are leaders guilty of under-delegation of responsibilities! A leader related that during the developmental phases of the ministry, he assumed many of the duties of administration in the Church. However, as the congregation grew and gifts of administration were added to the Church, he discovered that he was reluctant to release the authority over the administrative areas because he had functioned in them so long. He was obviously over-burdened with his responsibilities but was unwilling to delegate for fear of losing authority. As ministries grow, transitional periods occur during which there must be a decentralization of authority through delegation. If leaders fail to over haul their psyches and adopt a more effective leadership style, burnout is inevitable. Remember Moses and Jethro!

Ministry always holds challenges. The Apostle Paul made reference to his personal struggles with accusers, false brethren, and even the saints *(2 Cor. 11 & 12)*. Intimidation, fears, apprehensions, wonderment, rejections, failures, and reprisals represented a partial litany of experiences. It has been my experience that leaders can challenge the demonic powers, take on building programs by faith, preach and prophesy the Word of God to thousands of people without reservation. But personal enemies who seek to degrade their character and integrity can be the greatest challenge. Elijah challenged five hundred false prophets openly but fled from Jezebel *(I Ki. 19.1-3)*. David was a formidable leader and a man after God's own heart. He was fearless in the face of the enemies of his nation. Before Goliath, he was unrelentless and fearless *(1 Sam. 17:40-51)*. In the face of the bear and the lion that sought to attack the little sheep herd, he lacked no courage *(1 Sam. 17.36)*. But David, like most of us, did not handle his personal enemies very well. When the attacks were directed against his own character or threats upon his life, David reacted *(1 Sam. 25.5-35)*.

Personal challenges can cause even the most dedicated individuals to abandon their assignment. With this in mind, allow me to develop some of the reasons why people vacate their post.

1.   <u>Inability to move beyond personal hurts to a place of forgiveness and restoration</u>. Jeremiah the prophet voiced his complaint before the Lord: "O Lord, thou knowest: remember me, and visit me, and revenge me of my persecutors; take me not away in thy longsuffering; know that for thy sake I have suffered rebuke. Thy words were found, and I did eat them; and thy word was unto me the joy and rejoicing of mine heart: for I am called by thy name, O Lord of hosts. I sat not in the assembly of the mockers, nor rejoiced; I sat alone because of thy hand; for thou hast filled me with indignation. Why is my pain perpetual, and my wound incurable, which refuseth to be healed? Will thou be altogether unto me as a liar, and as waters that fail?" *(Jer. 15:15-18)*.

This may be self-vindication, self pity or simply the expression of the heart of a man in emotional distress. But the most significant part of this dialogue is the prescription given the prophet by the Lord: Therefore thus saith the Lord, if thou return, then will I bring thee again, and thou shalt stand before me: and if thou take forth the precious from the vile, thou shalt be as my mouth: let them return unto thee; but return not thou unto them. And I will make thee unto this people a fenced bronze wall: and they shall fight against thee, but they shall not prevail against thee: for I am with thee to save thee and to deliver thee, saith the Lord. And I will deliver thee out of the hand of the wicked, and I will redeem thee out of the hand of the terrible" *(Jer.15.19-21)*. The key phrase here is "if thou return." This illuminates the issue of continuation. No explanation for the pain nor the hurts is written. No praise of the prophet's suffering for the cause of the Lord is offered in Jeremiah's text. There is only the presentation of an option. If the prophet will recover himself and continue, then the promises of fulfillment of the mission are assured.

It is possible to identify with the lamentation of this prophet. Ministry holds a multitude of challenges. It is possible to get in such a mental state as to become paranoid, insecure, reclusive, and reluctant to express even personal feelings and desires. I encountered a leader of a growing Church who had been accused of improper management of the finances of a building project. The accusation proved to be false and unsubstantiated but the challenge left him wounded.

For months he ministered out of his wounds and devastation. Every Sunday during his preaching there would be some reference to the accusations. The experience had left dredges of resentment and bitterness which he poured out upon the congregation every Sunday. The individuals who made the accusations were still members of the congregation, and their presence simply served as a reminder of the incident.

To be erroneously accused of improper motives or any impropriety can be a devastating experience. To stumble in judgement and err in behavior can also be a source of embarrassment and shame. It can render a leader ineffective if there is an unwillingness to progress to a state of forgiveness.

2.   <u>Alienation</u>. Whenever a servant of God emphasizes some aspect of truth that he feels has been neglected, or he pursues a vision perceived to be of God, it can be expected that some will disagree. Some disagreement is helpful for it assists in the refining of the vision or the issue emphasized. However, some opposition is hostile and attacks the servant and the work as being unsound or lacking overall orthodoxy. The ultimate blow is the banishment of the individual in a kind of spiritual exile.

The Apostle John opens the book of Revelation with an interesting statement: "I John, who also am your brother and companion in tribulation, and in the kingdom and patience of Jesus Christ, was on the isle that is called Patmos, for the word of God, and for the testimony of Jesus Christ" *(Rev.1.9)*. John has been banished because his teaching and testimony did not meet the prevailing standards of orthodoxy. There is a striking cord of transcendency in John's statement of being "a brother and companion in tribulation." John, in my estimation, is identifying the fate of all who will be faithful in the discharge of their duties. They can expect to suffer public or private verbal abuse, accusation against their character, integrity, dedication, or allegiance. They can even expect an undermining of their accomplishments. However, leaving the ministry is not the solution.

All of us have basic psychological needs that we strive to fulfill. We want to be loved and cherished, accepted and respected by other people and especially our peers. Although these needs are common to everyone, they vary in importance for different individuals. The strength of these needs, and the manner in which they are satisfied or not satisfied, have significant implications on the decision making process. It is possible to become irrational in our response to negative activity directed our way. This possibility is greatly increased if we go into seclusion and exclude the participation of healthy counsel.

Self alienation creates an environment of fantasy and presumption that are sure to promote faulty conclusions and decisions. However, individuals who have close relationships with friends or family will have a relational resource to help them move successfully through such a period.

The problem encountered during such times may be real or imagined. The critical issue is simply this: will you make life changing decisions in this frame of mind and heart? Come out of your seclusion. Find a seasoned warrior who walks with a limp and has battle scars. Invite him or her to lunch. Eat more than just the natural food that is set before you. Be open and honest about your feelings. I am sure your guest will have some interesting stories to tell about their limp and scars.

3.   <u>Unwillingness to handle challenges, confrontations and criticisms.</u> There is a very interesting narrative contained within the third epistle of John. It appears that a certain Diotrephes has claimed authority that does not belong to him, and he has slandered the Apostle John. So the apostle declared: "I wrote unto the Church: but Diotrephes, who loveth to have the preeminence among them, receiveth us not. Wherefore, if I come, I will remember his deeds which he doeth, prating against us with malicious words: and not content therewith, neither doth he himself receive the brethren, and forbiddeth them that would and casteth them out of the Church" *(3 Jn 1:10.)* The apostle has well indicated his intentions to confront Diotrephes and to challenge the accusations.

Confrontation requires a tremendous emotional output. A litany of feelings ranging from fear, anger, and anxiety can be experienced. And if the personality dynamics of the individual is opposed to confrontational experiences, then the emotional turmoil is greatly increased. I encountered a pastor that loved confrontation. He was very argumentative and loved to debate. He seemed to thrive on the challenge. For many, however, a confrontational experience or a challenging meeting leaves them emotionally depleted.

In some instances fear of such emotional stress can cause an individual to avoid confrontation. Procrastination, delays, or failure to return phone calls or schedule meetings are signs of an avoidance reaction. In some instances, the anticipated anxiety can become so powerful that the individual will abandon a project or simply leave his post. A seasoned leader once related to me his reluctance to address the leadership and congregation of his Church concerning a building project. Since every previous building project had generated a crisis in the Church, the leaders and the people were strongly against any new project. At that stage in his life, he did not have the emotional reserve to confront the challenges or the criticisms that would certainly arise over the issue. He had decided to step down from the key leadership position and put the project in the hand of a younger associate. We discussed the matter at length. And we decided that he had two options: to obey or disobey what he considered to be a divine imperative. He decided that at this stage of his life he had more to lose by disobeying the Lord than obeying his self-protective instinct. The Book of Proverbs declares that "ointment and perfume rejoice the heart: so doth the sweetness of a man's friend by hearty counsel" *(Prov. 27:9)*. How often a dissenting opinion from a spouse or colleague can help us make the right decision.

4.   <u>Intolerance to change</u>. The willingness to overhaul our psyche and adapt to our environment is a virtue. This requires changing our patterns, perspectives, and in some instances, our value system.

We are very scripted to resist change or any reorientation upon the premise that it may be an admission of error or weakness. So we boldly use such mottos as "Resist the Devil" or "Stand fast." Foundation beliefs and conviction should be guarded against any encroachment, but there are times when it is a righteous thing to adopt a new pattern, embrace a different principle, or simply abandon a preconceived notion. The things which we may once have counted as gain, we may now declare lost in order to accomplish a goal set before us.

Be aware that there is no virtue in change itself. But resistance to growth and the assimilation of more knowledge is a claim of infallibility. It is a statement that we have arrived at perfection with no ground for improvement.

It seems apparent to me that whenever evil forces are at work upon an individual or a group there is a reluctance to change. There is a narrowing of consciousness of new ideas or concepts; a stifling of creativity, growth, and development; and a neurotic stagnation. The Holy Spirit seeks to promote interchange and encounter; encourages an environment that promotes creativity, growth, and development; and fosters a broader consciousness of other people, ideas, and concepts. Stubbornness and persistence are virtues in the pursuit of the stated will of God, but an intolerance to re-evaluate our principles, concepts, and methods is to claim that we are infallible. Let us search the Scriptures and be open to wise counsel, dialogue, and necessary change.

5.   <u>Lack of a true perspective of ministry</u>. A pastor of a very well known ministry related to me that he suffered a nervous breakdown during the earlier years of his ministry. His low self esteem and fear of failure drove him to work long hours visiting the sick, counseling, and serving on community organizations while attempting to nurture his own family. The drive to perform and succeed was a facade to hide his negative self-concept. When he failed or whenever others contributed to his failure, or when he was insulted in some way, he became angry . Unfortunately, rather than using the anger constructively, he suppressed it. The suppressed anger developed into deep resentment and depression. Because of his anxiety and fear, failure in any form became a source of self-condemnation and the disapproval of others. In this state of mind, he began to experience hopelessness and despair, and he eventually left the ministry for a while.

Whenever our self worth is built upon our ability to please others or upon our performance levels, we are destined for tremendous disappointment. Our self esteem must rest upon the love and forgiveness of Jesus Christ. This is still a simple but profound truth. That pastor will probably never fall into the performance trap, again and his current patterns indicate that he has a healthy sense of self appreciation.

Our concepts of ministry greatly determine our behavior. If ministry is performance, size of congregation, budget or popularity, then our behavior will support these entities. Natural needs will be subordinated to alleged "spiritual demands." The care of the physical and emotional man will suffer.

Ministry is not our performance. We are not productive simply because our appointment schedules are filled months in advance, nor because we are in demand around the clock. We are the ministry. If we are not emotionally, physically, and spiritually healthy, then the ministry is not healthy. We experience mountain top highs and valley lows. Success and failure, acceptance and rejection, clarity and perplexity will visit us. People will join us and leave us. If our perspectives of ministry are clear then our behavior will follow appropriately.

6.　　　　<u>Lack of definable goals or visions</u>. I was raised on a farm and learned to plow with a mule very early. My grandfather was a very successful farmer. Often I would see him plow a perfect furrow in a cleared piece of land without any rows or landmarks to guide his route. His explanation for his success at plowing beautiful, symmetrical rows in a field was very simple. He would set his sight upon a distant object such as a tree or stump and direct the mule in that direction. It worked every time. Visions or goals serve the same purpose or orientation. They focus our efforts and serve as a centripetal force to direct us toward a certain point. Visions or goals give purpose. Without some definable destination our efforts can easily become scattered and incoherent. Disappointment and despair can set in upon us if we don't know the road nor how far we have progressed. Be aware that visions are not gods. They are simply pictures, articulated dreams or signs that point us in the direction of the divine. They are landmarks that position us in time and space. We do not worship visions, for they are simply helpers or aids. The ultimate in life and service is to be conformed to the image and statue of Jesus Christ. So we have these landmarks to help facilitate that quest.

At the Cathedral of the Holy Spirit we were formulating our goal statement for the ministry several years ago. The leaders and staff had gathered together for two days of planning and evaluation. The leaders sensed a need to have a goal statement and some practical methods of attainment. We quickly discovered that some of the goals and visions would be immediate and some would be long range. There evolved a primary theme that seemed to arrest our discussion and evoke our complete agreement. Since that time, the articulation of that primary theme has served as a litmus test for every new evolving project or activity. We quickly discovered that visions can be pregnant and give birth to new ideas and concepts continually.

Whenever landmarks or vision are missing, there is an absence of restraints. There is no schoolmaster to tutor the students. And without productive guidance, irrational behavior will ultimately follow. Disappointment and disillusionment will not tarry far behind. We must open our hearts to the Spirit and the Word for constructive purpose and formulate visions and goals that will orient us and the ministry.

7.   <u>The declining dynamics of family and other contact groups</u>. A noted scientist said that the danger with too much knowledge is that you do not use it. We are prone to stumble over knowledge and wisdom. There are activities and practices, that we earnestly know should be a daily part of our life, but we neglect them. It is common knowledge that emotional exhaustion escalates when you get overly involved by taking on problems as your own, reacting to negative comments as if they were personal insults, and so on. We recognize that helping and caring for others requires good physical, emotional, and spiritual conditioning. We know that serving others requires that we ourselves have healthy social support from family, peers, and friends. Again, we have the knowledge, but we do not always use it for ourselves.

Getting away from people is a common response to stress and emotional overload. The desire for peace and privacy is desirable and understandable. The crisis occurs when getting away from others becomes excessive, and you cut yourself off from some valuable resources.

People can offer many things that you cannot secure for yourself---insights, information, emotional support, evaluation and feedback, advice and other valuable benefits.

Most of these can be provided by family or other contact groups such as peers or friends.

The family is a place of vulnerability, confidence, security, and love. A spouse or children can encourage, strengthen and provide checks and balances in your life. There is no greater opportunity to express your thoughts and feelings than when you are in the company of those who love and nurture you. You can be humorous and laugh and be yourself in the presence of family.

Small contact groups of peers or friends are also invaluable since they can offer a climate where honesty and vulnerability can flow. Wise men and women surround themselves with people who will be honest and open with them without intimidation. Praise, encouragement, positive and negative feedback from such associates can be very beneficial and possibly even save you from unhealthy decisions.

A noted leader once gave me some valuable insight for maintaining balance in life and ministry. He said to be careful when: (1) you think everyone is challenging or criticizing you; (2) you are not willing to express your ideas or concerns; (3) you escape from people and always feel compelled to isolate yourself; (4) you do not relate emotionally and sexually with your spouse any more; (5) you have an inclination not to fellowship with people or have a good time any more; (6) you feel pressed and emotionally drained most of the time; (7) you cry most of the time and lack control of your emotions (there is a difference between being touched by the Spirit of God and responding emotionally from being on the verge of an emotional breakdown); (8) you find your schedule is impossible to maintain; (9) you begin to think that food is sinful; and (10) you are not sleeping nor eating properly. When these symptoms escalate, a leader or any one that cares for others must be vulnerable to family or contact group of peers or friends. Do not hide these frustrations. Take advantage of the dynamics of family and close contact groups.

†   †   †

These factors apply to primary and secondary leadership. Hopefully we can benefit from the advantage others have because of experience.

Equipping and Training Laborers

Traditionally the care of souls has been delegated as a pastoral function consisting of the offering of the Word, sacrament, counsel, corrective guidance, and empathy. This function was generally the responsibility of the individual serving in the capacity of pastor. Yet the Biblical model of the Church is an equipping and enabling one which enlists the participation of the saints in the work of the ministry *(Eph. 4:4-16)*. Individuals who are not traditional pastors are enlisted to help administer care to the members.

This equipping and enabling model of the Church maintains the strengths of pastoral authority while providing a greater sharing in the responsibility of the caring of souls. It is a pattern where shared function is linked with giftedness rather than with a position or office. It allows people to exercise ministry and leadership within areas of gifts and callings.

Caregiving is being defined here as a holistic concern for the believers' physical, moral, spiritual well-being, growth, and sanctification *(1 Thess. 5:23)*. Salvation of the individual becomes more than the assurance of heaven and the cancellation of a fiery reservation. For the convert, it is a process of transformation, healing, and deliverance with hands-on ministry. There must be deliverance from fears, limitations, and snares that hinder the development of the potential and confidence of the individual. Stewardship and personal accountability must be taught. Finally there must be the enlistment of the believer's participation into a productive Christian community and the secular world.

Pulpit ministry alone cannot accomplish this process without the availability of auxiliary programs and support people. Innovative programs and instruction that provide opportunities for personal enrichment must be available. Decentralization of the leadership function becomes necessary to accommodate the demands of shepherding. Additional personnel becomes necessary to share in the ministry to the young, elderly, the singles, young families, single parents and the crisis-oriented members. As the process of decentralization occurs, each sub-ministry with its leadership becomes a new channel of influence and authority within the overall ministry. There is now the challenge of communication between the primal leadership function and the delegated functions. Ministry concepts and values must be imparted to this new group of leaders to ensure the ongoing integrity of the overall ministry.

We were at a critical period in the ministry of our Church and desperately needed help in the shepherding of the people. While we had an appropriate number of pastors, there was a need of hostesses, ushers, greeters, parking lot attendants, nursery workers, food technicians, audio and sound technicians, facility caretakers, home groups' leaders and a host of other workers to help shepherd the people. We discovered that the harvest was plenteous and the laborers were not few. So we sought to enlist the participation of a resource of workers among us without diminishing the strength of pastoral authority. We chose people who had integrity, potential, and a love for others. Their communication skills, talents, and abilities were secondary to their character.

A labor course taught by the pastors was offered to these workers as an aid to developing their ability to nurture people. The course did not focus on methods but on results. We were not interested in producing clones of the pastors. Our desire was to release the creative ability within these laborers to serve. The course was practical and theological and contained several basic elements:

1. What was to be accomplished and the expected accomplishment time.

2. Principles, concepts, or guidelines to be used.

3. Availability of resources to help achieve the ask.

4.   Method and time of evaluation of the work.

As pastors, we learned an invaluable lesson in the delegation of responsibility. People are more productive when they understand clearly what is expected of them. When they adequately comprehend the philosophy of the ministry, they can generate ideas and activities consistent with that philosophy. Whenever they were allowed to use their own creative initiative, it fostered an atmosphere of trust and confidence. By emphasizing principles and results rather than detailing a method, we were able to release delegated authority to perform the work of the ministry.

The delegation of authority is the delegation of responsibility and accountability. It is important that we discipline co-laborers to think. This is a process of supervised creativity which demands time and patience. But it will enlist the participation of the saints to do the work of the ministry, and that is the equipping and enabling model of the Church.

CHAPTER 3
THE CONCEPT OF AUTHORITY

"He that rules may occasionally serve; but He that serves will certainly rule."

"For though I should boast somewhat more of our authority, which the Lord hath given us for edification, and not for your destruction, I should not be ashamed; that I may not seem as if I would edify you by letters. For his letters, say they, are weighty and powerful; but his bodily presence is weak, and his speech contemptible." *(2 Cor. 10: 8-10).*

This passage lends itself to a discussion of the issue of authority. Authority in this instance is derived from the Greek word "exousia", meaning the rightful, actual, and unimpeded power to act, or to possess, to control, to use or to dispose of, something or somebody. The Apostie Paul declares that his "authority" has been derived from God and that its purpose is beneficial and not destructive. His critics have leveled a claim against him in asserting that "his bodily presence is weak, and his speech is contemptible." If that criticism were true, then there is no connection between Paul's authority and his natural physical attributes. His authority is not attributed to his eloquence nor to his over powering physical stature.

Authority and Revelation

In a Biblical sense authority is an issue of revelation. In the epistle to the Ephesians, Paul makes reference to a mystery made known unto him and other apostles and prophets that was not made known unto others before them *(Eph. 3:1-7)*. The revelation of this wisdom and knowledge by the Spirit has been a definitive source of their authority. If authority is the power to impart or to give, then one must of necessity have something of substance to render. Paul declares that he has received something from the Lord that empowers him "to make all men see what is the fellowship of the mystery, which from the beginning of the world hath been hid in God, who created all things by Jesus Christ." John declares in his epistle that the basis of his authority is "that which was from the beginning, which we have heard, which we have seen with our eyes, which we have looked upon, and our hands have handled, of the Word of life"*(1 Jn 1.1)*. Revelation by the Holy Spirit is the definitive source of Biblical authority.

There is the existing myth that authority is equated to volume or force or physical power. Therefore, Paul's critics questioned his "power" or "authority" since his bodily presence was weak and his speech was contemptible. If authority rests in the quality of the speech or in the strength of the physical stature, how could this man turn cities upside down and affect the religious climate of the day? There is a reference in Ecclesiastes 11 to a poor wise man who delivered a besieged city by his wisdom. Afterwards, no one remembered the poor man. The writer of Ecclesiastes concluded that wisdom is better than strength and the weapons of war even though wisdom is despised. There is an authority that is not comprehended by the unwise simply because it cannot always be measured. It is the authority of wisdom and knowledge. Since it is not always possessed by the eloquent or the strong, it is often negated or ignored. The race is not always won by the swift nor is the battle secured by the strong. There are so many occasions when the weak, the contemptible, and the unlearned possess a grace that surely comes from heaven. Unfortunately the writer of Ecclesiastes is correct when he declares: "The words of wise men are heard in quiet more than the cry of him that ruleth among fools" *(Eccl. 11:17)*.

Spiritual Authority

The Apostle Paul makes reference to an authority in the spiritual realm. He claims that we "wrestle not against flesh and blood, but against powers, principalities, against powers, against the rulers of the darkness of this world, against spiritual wickedness in high places" *(Eph. 6:12)*. To the Corinthian Church he writes: "For though we walk in the flesh, we do not war after the flesh; for the weapons of our warfare are not carnal, but mighty through God to the pulling down of strongholds" *(2 Cor. 10:3-4)*. There exists an authority in the spiritual realm of angels, demons, principalities, thrones, rulers of the darkness, and powers. This spiritual authority is power in the heavenly realm. It is the awareness of earthly influence in the heavenly sphere. The spirits declared to the seven sons of Sceva that they knew Jesus and Paul but did not recognize them *(Acts 19.14)*.

Authority is the activity of the Holy Ghost operating in the life of an individual. The exercise of the gifts of the Holy Spirit is indeed a demonstration of spiritual authority. Spiritual power is often demonstrated in prayer, preaching, teaching, writing, singing, and dancing. Such authority in these realms exhibits a significant effect upon people. It restores the fallen, heals the brokenhearted, and opens the prison doors of the captive. True spiritual authority promotes the praise and worship of God in a corporate body of believers, and it calls people to obedience.

Corporate Authority

Spiritual authority is displayed whenever God works with an individual, or a group. Often we witness this authority in an individual but there can be a corporate power that resides in a local work or ministry as a whole. This is the concept of corporate authority where a group or an entire congregation working together receives grace from the Lord. I have seen this principle demonstrated with musicians or singers who are quite effective as part of a local Church but become ineffective when they separate themselves from that assembly. A local Church can exhibit tremendous spiritual authority through all of its different ministries working together and lose it once fragmentation occurs. The same auxiliary ministries that were effective as part of a whole lose that virtue once they attempt to function independently of the parent body. It appears that there are some things that are intended to remain together in order to be productive.

Authority of Influence

There is the authority of influence which has the power to guide or manipulate somebody in a desired direction. For instance, a little maid who waited on the wife of Naaman influenced her mistress with information about divine resources in Samaria *(2 Ki. 5:1-4)*. Naaman was the captain of the host of the king of Syria and a man of significant power. He was afflicted with leprosy. The maid who spoke to the wife of this Syrian captain possessed no direct authority; however, she shared critical information at a precise moment. The availability of that information was the initiating factor in the healing of Naaman. Information influences decisions and can subject the hearer to choices, directions, and priorities. Those who possess information and share it with key people at strategic moments exert tremendous influence upon the decision making process.

The authority of influence is graphically exhibited in the example of a servant who knew how to approach an angry master. Once again it is the Syrian captain Naaman who has been enraged over the prescription given him by the Prophet Elisha *(2 Ki. 5:9-14)*. An unidentified servant approached Naaman and entreated him to follow the directions given by the prophet. The servant possessed no direct control nor office. However, the ability to approach and entreat this captain was the factor that influenced the decision.

There can be significant influence without control or ownership. A young pastor related to me his struggle over a decision regarding an influential position in the city. An opportunity to serve as mayor had been opened to him. It was apparent that a substantial support base was in place to ensure his election. He knew the position would give him the opportunity to control a significant portion of the city's government. After weeks of wrestling over the options, he was impressed with an interesting question: "Do you have to control or can you be content to influence?" That question settled the issue for him. He chose to maintain his pastorate, which included numerous political and social dignitaries, and he has served a most significant role.

Positional Authority

Positional authority is derived solely from the office or occupation. The actual power resides not in the individual but in the vocation. Secular Roman governors are described as God's servants to punish evil and encourage obedience to the law *(Rom. 13:1-6)*. While the governors may possess natural abilities to administrate, their authority is vested in the office they occupy.

Delegated Authority

Delegated authority is representative power. The apostles were Christ's commissioned witnesses, emissaries, and representatives *(Jn.17:18; Acts 1.8; 2 Cor. 5:20)*. They were given exousia by Him to found, to build up and to regulate His universal Church *(2 Cor. 10:8; 13:10)*. They gave orders and prescribed discipline in Christ's name *(2 Thessa. 3:6)*. They appointed deacons *(Acts 6:3-6)* and presbyters *(Acts 14.23; Titus 1.5)*. They presented their messages as Christ's truth, Spirit-inspired in both content and form of expression *(1 Cor. 2:9-13; Gal. 1:11-12)* as being normative for faith *(1 Cor. 14:37; 2 Thessa. 2.15)* and behavior *(2 Thessa. 3.6,14)*.

The Use of Authority

The use of authority is a critical issue. The Apostle Paul declared that the power given to him was beneficial and not destructive *(2 Cor. 10.8)*. Once the origin of the authority is established, there remains the critical issue of application. Even that which is divine in nature can be used contrary to its intended purpose.

Whenever authority is used inappropriately it stifles creativity, narrows consciousness, and promotes longstanding dependance -- which fosters immaturity. Misuse of authority frustrates the creative initiative of people to change or to improve their status. It restricts their awareness and makes them sectarian in thought and deed. It keeps the circle of association small not allowing any traffic in or out of designated boundaries. When the disciples of Jesus became aware that another person was ministering in the name of the Lord, they wanted to stop that work *(Lk. 9.49-50)*. Jesus rebuked their sectarian attitudes. On another occasion the disciples determined that the most appropriate response to a group of Samaritans was destruction *(Lk. 9.51-56)*. Once again the Lord reminded them that His authority had brought salvation, vision, and calling -- rather than destruction. The Lord was formulating the appropriate application of power. Whenever authority is used properly it generates life, growth, and expansion in those who are subject to it.

Authority is inappropriate when it is coercive and creates fear in those who are subject to it. Coercive authority generates dishonesty, suspicion, and deceit in both the leader and the follower. Whenever people act out of fear of reprisals or consequences, their commitment will be superficial and their loyalty will be short lived. Control and manipulation eventually generates anger, resentment, and retaliation from the victim. When open communication is discouraged and freedom of thought is imprisoned, frustration of the human will is inevitable.

Authority that is properly used will always promote integrity, honesty and trust because it benefits the common good of all involved. It stimulates creativity, broadens consciousness and fosters an atmosphere that promotes maturity. True authority allows for mistakes and growth. Since there is rarely growth without some mistakes, true authority promotes personal initiative through encouragement. Encouragement is most needed immediately after a mistake. Authority rightly used promotes self worth in others even when their performances fall short of the standard. True authority is based on a sense of equity and fairness. It encourages open and honest communication between the leader and the people. I marvel at the apparent open communication that existed between the Lord and the disciples. They demonstrated a given liberty to ask questions and to voice their opinions. The Biblical pattern seems to invite trust and cooperation.

The essence of all authority is benevolent service. The ultimate goal of power should be to benefit the welfare of others. It is vital that such a philosophy of authority be imparted to those who use it. Wherever authority is delegated, it is important that there be consistency in the nature and manner of its use. The delegates should represent in practice and philosophy the character of the Lord. In all of this there is a sense in which authority is substantiated. The Kingdom of God is not in word, but in power *(1 Cor. 4.20)*. I could say that authority is not in word, but in power. Paul declared to the Corinthians that his "speech and preaching was not with enticing words of man's wisdom, but in demonstration of the Spirit and power" *(1 Cor. 2.4)*. To those in the Corinthian Church who were boasting of their authority, Paul declared that he would soon discover if their alleged power rested solely in their eloquent speeches or true divine power *(1 Cor. 4.19)*. Wherever there is true Biblical authority, there is the fruit. When there was murmuring among the children of Israel, Moses took the rods of the pretenders of authority along with the rod of Aaron and placed them in the tabernacle of witness. Only the rod of Aaron budded & brought forth buds, and bloomed blossoms, and yielded almonds *(Num. 17:5-8)*. The fruitfulness of authority is verification in a Biblical sense. True authority will ultimately bear fruit. It will call the people of God to obedience and productivity.

CHAPTER 4

THE DYNAMICS OF TEAM MINISTRY
(Sharing The Anointing)

How can a plurality of leaders function together in fulfilling a single mission? A senior pastor related an incident in which a young associate came into his office and submitted a surprised resignation. The young associate was confident that the Lord had directed him in his decision. When the Pastor questioned him concerning his decision, it became clear that the young man was disappointed over his progress in the ministry. It appeared that the young Associate had joined the ministry with the hope of becoming the head of the music department. The expectations of this young man were beyond what the ministry could offer at his level of development. He resigned leaving a significant void in the leadership staff of that ministry.

Unrealized expectation can be a source of tremendous conflict. It seems advisable that the expectations and ambitions of associates be clearly known. Inappropriate expectations are fostered whenever there is a lack of clarity between what the ministry can provide and what associates expect.

Serving God often demands a corporate effort on the part of many people. Even a single pastorate generally requires elders, deacons, musicians, and other ministries of helps to facilitate the shepherding of the congregation. This collective action by a team of people requires some identification of function.

Function, as we know, is the purpose or action for which a person or thing is specially designed. This concept was so clearly demonstrated to me one afternoon by a colony of ants that had taken up residence in my yard. As I watched those tiny creatures performing their tasks, their effectiveness and productivity was quite obvious. There seemed to be a cooperative effort as I observed them moving in and out of their burrow. Although I was intrigued by their activities, I was not impressed by the damage done to my lawn by this large mound of excavated dirt. But it taught me a lesson. There is productivity in proper function. Whenever a person or thing is performing according to its designated function, there is productivity.

Prophets, Prophetic Ministry and the Pastorate

Ascension gift ministries of apostles, prophets, pastors, evangelists, and teachers have been set in the Church to equip the saints to do the work of the ministry. This occurs through teaching, disciplining and presenting a Biblical model that enables the saints to mature in character and lifestyle. The ultimate reality of this process is a people capable of producing the same character and lifestyle in others.

The gift ministries are called to facilitate the shepherding function of the Church. Shepherding is defined as a holistic concern for the believer's spiritual, moral well-being, growth, and sanctification. This caretaker function is not simply delegated to the pastor but is a collective responsibility of all of the ascension gift ministries. Although the nature of the ministry of the apostle, prophet, evangelist, and teacher may be different from that of the pastor, the collective goal is the edifying of the Church. Within a local Church the governing authority would be provided by a plurality of elders, who are resident in that congregation *(Acts 14.23, 15.2,4,6,22,23; 20.17,18; 21.18; Jam. 5.14)*. The authority of the elder is normally localized to the Church in which he/she is appointed. However, there are also the ministries of apostles, prophets, and teachers which are trans-local and can exercise authority wherever the Holy Spirit directs them within the Body of Christ.

The function of these trans-local ministries are to equip the saints to perform their tasks; to facilitate unity of the faith and right relationship among the believers; and to build up the Body of Christ *(Eph. 4.11-16)*. Whenever the trans-local ministries are functioning with the local elders, there should be a sense of mutuality and interdependence rather than a hierarchical relationship of apostles first, prophets second, teachers third, pastors fourth, and evangelist fifth. This five-fold group of elders may be local or trans-local, but they function in a cooperative and mutually submitted relationship to one another.

The effective ministry of the prophet must be a cooperative one. The prophet is not called simply to "root out, and to pull down, and to destroy, and to throw down." Such a limited concept of prophetic ministry omits the bipolar dimension of his/her work. For example, wherever there is an uprooting there is potentially a reinforcing; wherever there is annihilation there is the possibility of construction. The Jeremiah model of prophetic ministry did also include the responsibility to "build" and to "plant" *(Jer. 1.10)*. The prophet Haggai was used of God both to strongly rebuke and to exhort the same people *(Hag. 1-2)*.

Prophets functioning among pastors in a local Church serve among a plurality of elders. In the Church at Antioch there were certain prophets and teachers which functioned together with the local leadership, but they were also recognized as having specific ministries *(Acts 13.1)*. In respect of government, these men were on the same level with the other elders. But when functioning in their particular ministry, these prophets had a specific authority which their co-elders recognized. And likewise, the prophets recognized the authority of the local elders.

In a local Church the prophet and pastor should function in a non-competitive relationship. There must exist a mutual respect among the ministry of the pastor and prophet while acknowledging a leader of the group. In an instance where the senior leader is a pastor and the associate is a prophet, there can exist a cooperative and interdependent relationship if there is clarity concerning the ministering of spiritual gifts. It is the responsibility of the leadership to establish the government of spiritual ministry in a corporate gathering. This is not a difficult task once the purpose of a corporate gathering is established.

Paul gives some insight to the purpose of a corporate gathering in his epistle to the Church at Corinth: "Now, brethren, if I come unto you speaking with tongues, what shall I profit you, except I shall speak to you either by revelation, or by knowledge, or by prophesying, or by doctrine?" *(1 Cor. 14:6)*. This passage establishes several vital objectives of a corporate gathering:

1. Revelation

2. Knowledge

3. Prophesying (Edification, Exhortation and Comfort)

4. Doctrine

It appears that the corporate meeting of leadership and congregation is to serve several vital functions. Let us examine each of these individually:

1.   <u>Revelation</u>. In Christian thought this word expresses the self-disclosure of God to man. Revelation carries with it the idea of unveiling reviously hidden. It also suggests a visual appearance or manifestation of a deity.

      In a corporate gathering, it is the responsibility of leadership to illuminate the congregation through preaching and teaching. The source of the illumination is the Holy Spirit and the product is wisdom and knowledge given to the people in simple and practical language. Revelation is the communication of truth.

2.   <u>Knowledge</u>. This word connotes "a making known or giving of understanding that causes a person to come into obedient acknowledgment in their way of thinking and manner of living"

      Paul is not referring here simply to understanding that comes by objective observation of seeing, hearing, investigation, or experience. Nor is he relating simply to temporal understanding of such things as food, man-made laws, and regulations but to a full and real understanding of God as He revealed himself in the life and work of Christ. Paul acknowledges the Jews' zeal for God, but it is not in accordance with spiritual knowledge *(Rom. 10.2)*. The knowledge they lacked is the knowledge and recognition of God's ways. For it is not direct knowledge about God but knowledge of the unity of the Son with the Father, of his obedience, and his love as the one whom God sent.

3.   <u>Prophesying</u>. This word indicates divine inspiration in the proclamation of the will of God concerning an individual, a people, or a given situation. It means to make known, to declare or to speak as an oracle.

There are three benefits of this function. The *first function* is "edify" or "edifying" which means to build up or strengthen. In 1 Cor. 14, prophesying denotes the reinforcement of the faith and spiritual life of the Church. It is the elimination of confusion by enlightenment, and it results in productive behavior.

The *second function* of prophesying is exhortation, which denotes an urging of one to pursue some course of conduct. It means to influence the will, decision and behavior of another, or to call to one's side. In athletics, as well as in the Church, exhortation means to speak good words, to cheer up, to reassure, and to give hope in the face of challenge.

The *third function* is comfort which means to come along side of another, and to console and to stimulate someone to discharge their duties.

4.   <u>Doctrine</u>. This word connotes education, instruction, and the impartation of systematic, fundamental learning. It seems apparent that when the purpose of a corporate assembly is understood, the extremes, wrong emphasis, or operational errors can be eliminated. Furthermore, there can exist a productive and mutual relationship between all of the ascension gift ministries.

†   †   †

Conflicts and controversies surrounding prophetical ministry in a local Church is most often attributed to immaturity and lack of a definitive ministry philosophy. That is why the effective ministry of a prophet is cooperative, as stated earlier. A senior pastor related to me his fear of prophetic ministry because of some experiences. He had allowed a prophet to minister in his local assembly with devastating results. The visiting prophet had ministered the Word quite effectively but during the time of personal ministry there arose some controversy. A young man in the congregation was openly accused of being a homosexual and the minister of music was rebuked quite harshly.

The answer to such conflicts and controversies regarding prophetic ministry is not disuse but the establishment of proper spiritual protocol that is Biblically valid and situationally specific for that local congregation. Spiritual ministry must be kept within the context of the order and content of the worship experience. Because worship is a reenactment or recitation of historical events, it becomes necessary that the creeds, hymns, preaching, teaching, prophesying, and all spiritual ministry be held in a managed, wise balance with the overall purpose of our interaction with God. This may be an answer to imbalances or operational irregularities that potentially can occur during any worship experience. And finally, the prophet and pastor must communicate and act upon all previously discussed principles.

CHAPTER 5

CONFLICTS, PROBLEMS & RESOLUTIONS (CPR)

WHENEVER PEOPLE work together for a common mission, conflict inevitably arises. This is particularly true in ministry. Decisions are made and actions are taken that have tremendous psychological and practical implication. In Acts 6, a conflict arose between the Grecians and the Hebrews over the distribution of provision among the widows. The solution to the problem was the delegation of seven honest men, full of the Holy Ghost and wisdom to handle the distribution and daily service of the table. The conflict presented an opportunity for the Apostles to solve a ministerial problem by the delegation of leadership based upon gifting and function.

The Apostle Paul makes reference to the daily care of the Churches, the challenges, and difficult situations he faced. There were theological issues to be challenged and corrected *(Gal. 3-4; Col. 2: 2 Thessa. 2)*; gifts of the Holy Spirit being used for vain display *(1 Cor. 14)*; strife of theological factions and sectarian animosities *(1 Cor. 3)*; and disunity between members in the same Church (Phi. 4). Let us mention again the Apostle John's reference to a certain Diotrephes who refused to recognize the authority of the Apostle *(3 Jn)*. In addition to these there were false apostles, prophets and teachers who actively perverted the truths of the gospel *(Acts 13:6; 2 Cor. 11:13; Gal. 2:4; 2 Peter 2:1)*. Magicians and spiritualists bewitched many people *(Acts 8:9; 13:8)*.

The Church of this century faces similar challenges: conflicts within and without, false leaders, erroneous doctrines, and even psychic phenomena. Equally threatening are also problems involving ethics and government. Let's examine some examples that could potentially exist in any ministry.

Case 1a

A senior pastor has discovered that his music director is homosexual. The young musician has been a tremendous support to the music ministry and a very capable leader. Two of the elders of the Church have recommended that the young man confess his faults before the entire congregation and step down from ministry. The senior pastor, having spoken at length with the young man, feels that a public confession would be punitive and greatly hamper the ability of the congregation to respond favorably to the young man in the future. The elders are insistent and are threatening to bring the issue before the entire congregation.

Case 2a

Several business people in a local Church have approached the senior pastor concerning a very lucrative plan. It is a multi-level marketing program that promises significant revenue to the Church if the pastor will give support to it and encourage the congregation to participate. The pastor feels reluctant over using his office and the pulpit to endorse a business plan of any type. He decides not to endorse the plan and encourage the business people to operate their work outside the campus of the Church. This creates quite a stir, and several of the business people threaten to leave.

Case 3a

A senior pastor is being strongly encouraged to adopt a congregational form of government for the local Church. Two of the three elders are in favor of this change. The pastor discovers that the motivation behind the entire movement is the associate pastor who desires to shift leadership from the senior pastor to a voting congregation which will eventually affirm a new pastor. The Church currently functions under a plurality of elders with the senior pastor serving as the leader.

Case 4a

Pastor Bill is a very gracious man and willing to accept any ideas and concepts that will profit the Church. The Sunday morning services are becoming very challenging to him. The music leader keeps the congregation standing for over an hour singing. Members from the congregation are being encouraged to stand spontaneously to prophesy. Pastor Bill does not desire to be authoritarian but the course of events are getting out of hand. Some members are coming to him and complaining about standing so long. Others are afraid of the lack of control in the meetings. He is distressed over the issue because he desires freedom and order and wonders if both are possible.

Case 5a

A local, ethnically homogeneous Church is undergoing a significant change in the congregation. Blacks, Whites, Orientals and Hispanics are beginning to worship together. Initially tremendous excitement surrounds the dynamics of this new experience. There exists a mutual accommodation and cultural interchange among the group. Different idioms of musical expressions are introduced.

Gradually, the cultural tolerance begins to diminish. Group preferences begin to surface, becoming more obvious during times of corporate worship. Ethnic and cultural responses to the different kinds of musical selections become obvious. Efforts to appease the musical requirements of each group become less successful. Thus the musical department experiences some difficulties because the different ethnic groups are requesting to sing more of "their kind" of music.

Case 6a

Pastor Teresa has recently attended a conference that attracted thousands of people. There were workshops, discussion sessions during the day and a tremendous display of books, tapes and resource materials. The night sessions were charged with excitement and enthusiasm. There were spiritual manifestations among the platform leaders and among the congregation. People were leaping, running, shouting, dancing and laughing almost uncontrollably.

Several of the pastor's elders and members were also attending the conference. Several weeks later Pastor Teresa was approached repeatedly by members of the congregation and two of the elders requesting to meet with her about the conference. They all wanted to experience the excitement and events of that conference in their local Church.

Case 7a

The public media has printed numerous stories concerning ethical and moral violations by Church leadership. Radio and television talk show hosts are featuring daily programs targeting the failure of Church leadership. Such a public exposure of the crisis among Church leadership has created a general atmosphere of mistrust and suspicion. As a result, non-Church coalition groups are being created to influence legislation designed to protect congregants from spiritual and emotional abuse. Laws are being fashioned to control pastoral counseling and to provide strict discipline of Church leadership found guilty of moral and ethical charges involving congregational members.

In addition to the leadership crisis issues, the Christian community is decisively divided over the issue of abortions. The divergent poles of "pro-life" and "pro-choice" have literally divided the Church community.

In the midst of such a religious and social climate, a local pastor has been notified of the moral misconduct of his associate pastor. The associate pastor professed his innocence but the elders are calling for a full scale investigation by an outside non-partisan board. One of the elders has notified the media. This all occurred on Thursday, and Sunday is coming. The senior pastor must address a sensitized congregation on Sunday morning.

†   †   †

Several of these scenarios would have been foreign to the Church years ago. But today, the crisis of leadership, multi-culturism, Church government issues, spiritual protocol, multi-level marketing, fads and spiritual reformation represent a litany of challenges and conflicts faced by Church leadership. Some of these issues may very easily be labeled as simply distractions and deterrents by some observers. Others may choose to deal with them as "spiritual matters" and wage spiritual warfare. Regardless of the assessment, these are issues with both spiritual and natural significance.

There are several approaches that have been used by various leadership models depending upon their theological background. The reader is encouraged to record a treatment of each case in the space allotted. Several of these are presented:

Case 1b

<u>Issues:</u>　　　　Personal lifestyles and moral responsibilities of leadership; philosophy of restoration.

<u>Resolution A</u>: The pastor removed the musician from his post after a public confession and designated a specific period of time for counseling and possible restoration. If recovery is successful, the musician must come before the elders and congregation and acknowledge his true repentance and restoration.

<u>Reasoning A</u>: Lev. 18:22, 1 Ki. 15:11-12, Rom. 1:26-27, 1 Cor. 5:1-7.

<u>Resolution B</u>: The musician is not removed from his post nor is there a public confession. The restoration of the of the young musician will be handled by the pastor and a designated counselor for a prescribed period of time. The young man is assigned to a support group.

<u>Reasoning B</u>: *Lev. 18:22, 1 Ki. 15:11-12, Rom. 1:26-27, 1 Cor. 5:1-7, Gal. 6:1.*

Even though the young man's ministry is public, the issue at hand is a private one that should be handled by spiritual eldership. Public exposure of such would only draw attention to the matter and have a negative effect upon the restorative process. A careful consideration of the willingness of the young man to receive help, the availability of pastoral counsel and a ministry support group justifies such an approach.

<u>Resolution C</u>:

<u>Reasoning C</u>:

Case 2b

Issues:
Private business on Church property; public endorsement of individual business concerns.

Resolution A:
No personal for profit business shall be permitted on the Church campus. This shall be established as a ministry philosophy and the by-laws of the Church shall reflect such a decision.

Reasoning A:
The Church is a non-profit organization and should not permit "for profit" business endeavors to operate on its campus. If the pulpit is used to endorse personal businesses of members it will create a precedent obligating such announcements for all such future concerns of any member. The leadership of the Church must maintain the authority establishing operational principles. Tithes and offerings are still valid support vehicles for the Church. The business people shall operate business off the campus of the Church without public endorsement.

Resolution B:
Allow public announcement of business opportunities without the endorsement of the Church. Such announcement shall be made by a representative of the business community and a copy shall be printed in Church bulletin.

Reasoning B:
The Church should endorse the business endeavors of its members. This fosters the development of a business community and encourages the members of the congregation to support them. A Christian business organization should establish a directory of its members and circulate it freely among the congregation. The Church should do business with itself.

Resolution C:

Reasoning C:

Case 3b

Issues: Crisis management and Church government.

Resolution A: The Church shall continue to function with a plurality of elders and the senior pastors serving as leader. The by-laws reflect such a government and will not be changed. The elder will be brought before the presbytery.

Reasoning A: In New Testament congregations, all members or disciples were expected to be under the authority of appointed leaders. These leaders were referred to collectively as elders, overseers or shepherds *(Acts 11:30, 14:23, 15:2,4,6,22,23, 20:17, 1 Thesa. 5:12, 1 Tim. 5:17, Titus 1:5,7, Heb. 13:7,17,24.)* There is no scriptural validation for a congregation to rule or direct the affairs of the Church.

Resolution B: The Church shall continue to function under a plurality of elders with the leadership of the senior pastor. However, when necessary certain members of the diaconate shall sit with the presbytery.

Reasoning B: *Acts 6:1-6, Phi. 1:1.* Since the presbytery has the responsibility of directing the affairs of the Church it is wise for it to provide channels of input from all levels of the ministry.

Resolution C: _______________________________
                    ____
                    ____
                    ____

Reasoning C: _______________________________
                    ____
                    ____
                    ____

Case 4b

Issues: Spiritual protocol and philosophy of ministry.

Resolution A: The senior pastor is ultimately responsible for every service and as the chief shepherd will determine, in collaboration with the worship leader, what is appropriate.

Reasoning A: *1 Cor. 12, 14, Rev. 4-5.* The meeting that takes places between God and His people is always based on the Word, prayer, and the sacrament. The ingredients of worship cannot be left to the whims of creative people. If worship is a dramatic re-enactment of biblical, historical events there must be a script, a director, a time frame and proper participation of the congregation. Worship can be structured and free. If the principle of edification is not violated it can be done decently and in order with all members of the congregation profiting from their interaction with God.

Resolution B: The worship leader is responsible for the ministry of music and singing.

Reasoning B: Musicians are talented and very sensitive. They should be allowed to direct their portion of the service with the same degree of liberty that the Pastor has in preaching the word.

Resolution C: _______________________________

Reasoning C: _______________________________

Case 5b

<u>Issues:</u> Prejudice and multi-culturalism in religious and social expressions.

<u>Resolution A:</u> *Acts 2:1-21, Gal. 3:28, Rev. 5:9-10,7:9, 14:6.* There will be no toleration of fragmentation of the Church. God-centered worship shall transcend ethnic-centered worship. There is a delicate balance between God-centered worship and the praise and musical preferences of the congregation.

<u>Reasoning A:</u> Worship is christocentric and not ethnocentric. It acknowledges and recapitulates the historical, present, and future events of Christ Jesus in the redemption of the individual and the cosmos. Biblical worship is a personal meeting with God. Therefore, the ingredients of worship (creeds, music, preaching, and teaching) are not arbitrary nor are they controlled by ethnic demands. Since public worship is both individual and corporate, edification of the whole Church shall be the major consideration in the selection of music. The pattern is the singing of "hymns, spiritual songs and making melody in your (personal or ethnic) hearts." Accommodation, not competition, shall be the code.

<u>Resolution B:</u> Cultural and ethnic expression should be enhanced with opportunity given for musical selections representing each group. Diversity shall transcend accommodation.

<u>Reasoning B:</u> Expressions in worship should be "all things to all people." Focusing upon the ethnic and cultural needs in worship will acquaint the entire congregation to the different expressions.

Resolution C:

Reasoning C:

Case 6b

Issues: Spiritual protocol, fads and reformations.

Resolution A: Invite several of the conference speakers to the Church and expose the general congregation to the teaching and the experience.

Reasoning A: The Church should maintain an "open pulpit."

Resolution B: Establish a clear protocol for spiritual manifestation in the local Church. Distinguish teachings and practices that are foundational to the faith from those that are supportive.

Reasoning B: Ministries must be established upon proper foundations. Emotionalism and excitement without some order and directives will ultimately prove to be counterproductive.

Resolution C: _______________________________

____

____

____

Reasoning C: _______________________________

____

____

____

Case 7b

<u>Issues</u>:   Judicial responsibilities of elders and public disclosure

<u>Resolution A</u>: Relieve the minister of his responsibilities pending a full scale investigation by a non-partisan board of elders and public statement to the congregation.

<u>Reasoning A</u>: Since the issue is of public record, there must be some public disclosure of the treatment of the matter. Since local   elders can be bias in their opinions and judgment of a colleague, a trans-local group of elders would be more objective. Also such a board would dispel any suspicion among the congregation concerning the resolution of the matter.

<u>Resolution B</u>: Do not relieve the minister of any responsibilities. The senior pastor and the local eldership shall bear the responsibility of resolving the matter. A public statement shall be made by the senior pastor regarding the alleged incident and the violation of protocol in the public disclosure of any untreated issue involving an elder or a member of the congregation.

<u>Reasoning B</u>: The judicial responsibility of local eldership is to rule. Since elders are trained in both Biblical law and covenant responsibilities and are experienced in compassion, it is not beyond their capabilities to judge and restore one among their own ranks. Public disclosure of such an issue must be with the consensus of the local elders and not a unilateral decision of one elder.

Resolution C:

Reasoning C:

CONCLUSION

For any ministry to survive, there must be a commitment to Biblical principles and the existence of some consistency in ministry philosophy among leadership and congregation. The dynamics of failure and success need to be understood within the context of environmental influences along with the physical, psychological, and spiritual state of the individual, and the motive and overall influence or implication to the corporate Church. And finally, there must be a commitment between primal leadership, associates and staff to work in a mutually interdependent manner to treat any issue that threatens the productive continuity of the Church.

About the Author

Dr. Kirby Clements is an associate pastor at the Cathedral of the Holy Spirit in Atlanta, Georgia. He travels extensively throughout the United States and the Nations as liaison to Archbishop Earl Paulk.

Dr. Clements earned his Bachelor of Science degree from Morehouse College, D.D.S. from Howard University and his post-doctorate, M.Sc.D. from Boston University.

He is the author of A Philosophy of Ministry which speaks to the role of the church in a contemporary society and soon to be published, Discernment.